Dragonfly: A Lancaster Novel
Book 1
Stacy Goforth

STACY GOFORTH
author

Stacy Goforth

Library of Congress Control Number: 2025906291

Paperback ISBN: 979-8-9985002-0-6

eBook ISBN: 979-8-9985002-1-3

Book Design: by Stacy Goforth

First edition 2025

For my husband Gary, for responding with an exasperated blush as you read each chapter, for tirelessly listening to me ramble about characters in my head, and for supporting me every step of this journey. You will forever be my love story.

For my daughter Felicia, for all your wonderful & terrible ideas that you contributed to this story, but most of all, I hope this proves to you that if you put your mind to it, you can accomplish anything.

"There is a sacredness in tears. They are not the mark of weakness, but of power. They speak more eloquently than ten thousand tongues. They are the messengers of overwhelming grief, of deep contrition, and of unspeakable love."

Washington Irving

Small Town — John Mellencamp · 3:42

What's Love Got to Do with It — Tina Turner · 3:47

Thanks fr th Mmrs — Fallout Boy · 3:24

Uptown Girl — Billy Joel · 3:18

Time After Time — Cindi Lauper · 4:01

Livin' on a Prayer — Bon Jovi · 4:09

I Don't Wanna Miss a Thing — Aerosmith · 4:59

Love is a Battlefield — Pat Benatar · 4:05

You Outta Know — Alanis Morissette · 4:09

Welcome to the Jungle — Guns N' Roses · 4:33

So High School — Taylor Swift · 3:49

Crush — Cigarettes After Sex · 4:27

Save a Horse (Ride a Cowboy) — Big & Rich · 3:20

Bad for Business — Sabrina Carpenter · 3:08

Home — Foo Fighters · 4:53

Thunderstruck — AC/DC · 4:53

Dicktionary

Here for the smut? Skip this page and read on...

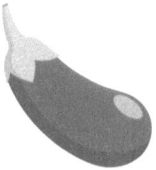

Feeling shy? Feel the need to skip through the more steamy scenes? Below is a list of chapters with sexual content so you are aware ahead of time:

Chapter Eight
Chapter Ten
Chapter Eleven
Chapter Twelve
Chapter Fifteen
Epilogue

Happy reading...

Chapter One

Samantha

S amantha Lancaster did not cry.

Not that she was incapable of producing tears. Her glands worked appropriately. It was rather that she found it all arbitrary. Nothing good in Sam's life had ever come from crying.

Tears couldn't retrieve Mr. Jangles after the Oil Creek incident when she was three. It never healed a single scratch, and it didn't bring her mother back after she died of cancer on her sixth birthday.

Her father used to say to her, *"You never cry over spilled milk, striking out at the plate, or taxes."*

No matter how much she wanted to cry over her damn taxes each year. Being an adult sucked.

Driving down I-8, she stared out the window at the peaceful landscape in front of her. The leaves on the trees had finally finished merging into their vibrant shades of orange and red. The serene view on the other side of the glass had been a deep contrast to the phone call from her brother, Dylan, last night. His call wasn't unexpected given their frequent conversations, but the crack in his voice at the immediate mention of their eldest brother had let her know quickly that something was wrong.

It was because of Jackson that she was turning onto Central Avenue and heading to Titusville Area Hospital before dawn on an early October Thursday morning. He had crashed his motorcycle out on Church Run Road sometime last night and the hospital wasn't giving out any information over the phone on his condition.

Leave it up to Jackson to always know how to get her attention and send her racing back home.

She parked her vintage yellow Volkswagen Bug at the back of the parking lot and looked up at the old hospital. Nothing ever changed around this place.

Damn, she really hated hospitals!

She barely made it into the waiting room before Dylan was out of his chair and embracing her in one of his famous "Dilly Bear" hugs that reminded her of home. "How's Jackson?" she asked, noticing from the way his eyes appeared bloodshot, and his hair was unkept, that he must not have slept all night.

Dylan was a full two years older than her. Sam had struggled to say his full name as a child, but they were thick as thieves when they were growing up. The two of them would run off and hide from their older brother Jackson, giggling until he found them under the stairs. After playtime, Dylan would head off with his older brother, and Sam would chase after him, begging for her "Dilly

Bear" hugs. Though he forbid her to call him that in public now, it was still lovingly his nickname on her phone.

She gazed, noticing that his voice was hoarse. "The goddamn nurse keeps saying they'll update us soon, but they never do."

She knew she would need to work to calm her brother. "I'm sure they would tell you if they knew anything, Dylan."

Her father stood up, and she couldn't help but notice a few more gray hairs lining his beard since the last time she had been home. "Hey, Daddy," she said, greeting him with a hug.

"How was the drive, Dragonfly?" She immediately picked up on his anxiety, despite his attempt to disguise it with the playful nickname.

No one else called her that. It was a nickname she earned when she was four years old, while camping down at old Oil Creek. She had wandered off, chasing a dragonfly, not a care in the world. She didn't realize she was lost until she found herself next to a rock by the creek, holding her bunny, Mr. Jangles. Hours later, her father found her sitting on that rock, tears in her eyes, Mr. Jangles lost to the creek, and a dragonfly sitting on her sleeve. Not only did the nickname stick, but its continued use was underscored by the profound love her mother had always had for dragonflies, creatures she held most dear among all others. She was certain that was the reason the name still held a significant connection with her father.

Nuzzling into her dad now, the familiar smell of leather and cigarettes surrounded her. She knew she'd have to talk to him about quitting smoking again, but perhaps now wasn't the best time. "You know how Pittsburgh traffic is in the morning." She shrugged. Traffic was probably the one thing she hated about living in the city.

Her father grumbled under his breath, "It's the fucking inflation."

Dylan ran his hand through his hair. "Dad, inflation has nothing to do with the traffic."

"Have you seen the cost of gas, boy?" his father said with a quick smack to the back of his head.

Just then, a woman who appeared ready to end her shift stood in the doorway, holding a clipboard. "Lancaster?" she called out.

Like moths to a flame, they swarmed her. "How is he?" they asked in unison.

"Well, he's lucky he was wearing a helmet," she said with a laugh. However, her laughter faded when she realized that none of them found it appropriate to joke. "Anyway, he's pretty banged up. He has a torn rotator cuff, a couple of broken ribs, and second-degree road rash that's going to sting. But the worst injury seems to be his broken leg."

"All of that seems pretty fucking bad," Dylan said to the nurse before their father gripped his shirt to interrupt him.

"Excuse my boy, I raised him in a barn, apparently. Zero manners. Please continue."

The woman smiled at her father, appreciating his interruption, and resumed speaking. "He broke his right leg in four places. I'll let Doctor Roberts explain the details, but it will require surgery."

"Can we see him?" Hospitals had never been a place of comfort for her. Her mother had spent so much time in them when Samantha was a child that she always felt they robbed her of precious time she would never get back.

"He's not awake yet, but once the doctor talks to you, I should be able to take you back. However, only two people at a time," the woman said, stepping away from them.

The hospital seemingly enjoyed making her wait. Corporate fucking bloodsuckers in white lab coats.

Her brother's nervous pacing in the waiting room gave her a headache. Dylan was the least patient of the Lancaster children. She chalked it up to him being the middle child. Not being first born or the baby of the family, Dylan always got frustrated waiting for his turn or trying to get their father's attention in everything he did.

Something about Dylan's behavior was bothering her. "Can you please sit down? You're making me dizzy."

"I just don't understand what he was doing all the way up on Church Run," he said, mostly to himself. "It doesn't make any sense. He told me he was going back to the shop, and that's on the other side of town."

"He wasn't drinking, was he?" She didn't want to have to ask, but she knew her brothers. They weren't saints, but their reputation in town was slightly exaggerated. However, she knew they liked to have a few beers at Boondock's after work to blow off steam.

"It was just one beer, Sam," he said. "You know Jax, he could still sing the National Anthem after one beer."

"He can't even do that sober." Their dad glanced upward in frustration and stood up to check in at the nurse's station one more time.

Once they were alone, she looked her brother in the eye. "God's honest truth, he wasn't drunk?" she asked.

"I swear, he was fine when he left the bar. He told me he was going to the shop. I have no clue what he was doing up on Church Run," he said, pinching his fists together.

Sam realized that something was off. "Obviously he didn't go to the shop, or Dad would have said something."

Dylan took a seat next to her and leaned closer. "Dad's been acting weird, not just today. I don't know what it is, but Jax was upset last night," he said in a tight whisper.

Curious, she lowered her own voice. "Weird how?" Peering around a pole, she searched for their father, while Dylan absent-mindedly picked at the mud on his boots.

"Jax thinks something is going on with the shop. He was going over there to talk to him last night," Dylan said, as if he was revealing some sort of dirty secret.

Sam couldn't stop her laughter. What in the conspiracy theory bullshit was he trying to say? She leaned forward, covering her mouth with her hand. "Do you think Dad tried to take him out, Dyl?"

Annoyed, Dylan threw his hands up in the air. "Dammit, Sam, that's not what I'm saying."

Sam reached into her bag and pulled out a hair clip, securing her curly brown hair on top of her head. As she twirled a few tendrils, she asked, "Then what are you trying to say?"

Concern filled Dylan's voice as he responded, "I just think it's strange that Jax mentioned talking to Dad about his behavior last night. And now he's lying in a hospital bed, broken, and I don't know why."

"I'm sure he'll explain it when he wakes up."

Dylan stared at her, wide eyed. "*If* he wakes up."

Dylan Lancaster, pessimist extraordinaire, ladies and gentlemen.

She reached over and took his hand, gently dragging it into her lap. Despite being two years younger than her brother, she was always the one taking care of him. Even after she moved to Pittsburgh four years ago, Dylan still texted her every morning, sharing details about his previous day or tattling on something Jackson had gotten into that week. Deep down, she knew Dylan saw her moving away as an act of betrayal, even though he would never admit it.

Their dad returned from the nurse's station; a look of concern evident on his face as he spoke. "Doc says they are going to take him in for surgery soon to repair his femur."

Dylan's grip tightened on her hand. "Can we see him first?"

"He's not awake, but I think they'll let you and Sam go back." Dylan nearly sprinted toward the nurse's station before she even left her seat.

"You sure you don't want to go?" she asked. "I can wait out here."

"Nah, I've seen the inside of a hospital room more times than I'd like to count. Keep him out of trouble, will ya?" His eyes trailed toward her brother, pacing nervously as he waited with the nurse.

"As if that's ever been possible," she said before shaking her head and leaving her father alone in the waiting room.

She and Dylan stood on opposite ends of the elevator, staring at the lights above the door as each one lit up, signaling the floor that brought them closer to Jax's location. As a child, she felt scared and small, holding her father's hand as she waited to see her mother. She stepped closer to her brother, sliding her hand into his as the elevator door opened, alerting them to their arrival in the post-op wing.

She felt unprepared for what awaited her as she entered Jax's hospital room. The buzzing of fluorescent lights assaulted her ears, blending with the constant beeping of the monitors. The overwhelming smell of antiseptic filled her nostrils, making her instantly nauseous.

Her brother lay motionless in the hospital bed, his face marred with blood and scratches. She was certain the gash across his chin would leave a scar.

She could already hear him justifying how it made him look more rugged. *"Scars are sexy, Sam."* Wasn't that what he always told her when she fell and scraped her knee?

The tubes and wires connecting him to the machines looked intimidating, making his over six-foot frame seem small. "You look like shit, bro," Dylan said, wrinkling his nose in fake disgust.

"He's gonna love hearing you tell him that."

"Then maybe he should get up and do something about it." Dylan stood by the bed, staring down at their brother's broken body. She wrapped her arm around Dylan's waist and, with her other hand, squeezed Jackson's exposed hand.

They stood there in tense silence; the room filled with a heavy stillness that suffocated the air. With each tick of the clock, the urge to flee grew stronger, a piercing reminder of the uncertainty that hung in the air.

It was almost a welcome reprieve when Doctor Roberts came to collect him for surgery. She kissed his forehead, pausing only to whisper her final warning against his cheek. "Don't do anything stupid, loser."

Dylan stood like a stoic statue next to her as they wheeled him away, not wanting to move until the doors to the O.R. closed behind him.

"We should go back down and update Dad," Samantha said, her stomach growling from hunger by the time they got back to the waiting room.

The drive from Pittsburgh to Titusville was only two hours. However, she had left without eating breakfast, which for Sam meant just a small box of Fruit Loops and a soda. This morning, though, she had so much on her mind that she left without eating.

She went off in search of a snack machine, hoping to find something to fill the pit of anxiousness at the bottom of her stomach. Immediately, her eyes were drawn to the bag of Funyuns on the top row. Sadly, she also noticed the coin slot on the side of the machine.

She had forgotten what it was like to be in a small town. Living in Pittsburgh had been an adjustment for her. However, not all the changes were bad. One of her favorite things about living in the city was moving into an apartment where she could see the sunrise from her bedroom. Not that she couldn't see a sunrise in Titusville, but opening her blinds and sitting on her bed in front of the giant bay windows as she overlooked the river while the sun came up over the water was something she couldn't describe. It was one of those "guess you had to be there" moments that she couldn't explain to her brothers.

She had also gotten used to the fact that she could go out after 9:00 PM, and stores would still be open where she could grab a pizza at 3:00 AM and no one would bat an eye about it.

Living in the city came with other conveniences too. She had grown accustomed to being able to use her debit card for her quick fixes from the snack machines at work, but the ones in Titusville only took cash.

She shoved her hands into her pockets, pulling out a few coins and some lint. "Piece of shit." Frustration overwhelmed her as she kicked the base of the machine.

Behind her, she heard a light chuckle and then the sound of a voice she hadn't heard in years.

"Not sure you'll get anywhere with that attitude."

One hand went to rest on her hip as the other absentmindedly reached for the hair at the nape of her neck.

Blake Forrester, the object of every single fantasy she had ever had since she was twelve, was standing behind her and she looked like a drowned rat.

It would be just her luck that she would look like she had been through a tornado, because why the hell not? She turned at the waist, a pair of caramel brown eyes staring back at her. "I don't carry change with me anymore," she said, her voice accompanied by a strangled laugh that made her skin crawl.

"Four years turn you into an unprepared city girl, Sam?" Blake dug into his pockets, producing the coins needed for the machine. "Still eat those disgusting Funyuns?"

She nodded, trying not to giggle and twirl her hair like an idiotic schoolgirl whose high school crush just remembered her favorite snack.

As Blake moved to retrieve the bag from the machine, she couldn't help but stare at him as he bent over, even though she knew she shouldn't. He was still as handsome as ever. His brown hair with his slightly messy curls looked as if he had been running his hands through his silky locks, the way the strands stuck up in every direction. More likely, he had a girlfriend to do that for him. She couldn't imagine him still being single.

She suspected her intense reaction to Blake's appearance stemmed from the stress of Jackson's condition and her lack of sleep. It had been years since she'd even thought about Blake Forrester. High school crush, unrequited love...

Her brother, Dylan, approached them. "There you are."

Oh yeah, in case she had forgotten all the other reasons it had never worked out for her and Blake, the world had conspired against her and also made him her brother's best friend.

Chapter Two

Blake

B lake Forrester was pretty sure that people would consider him easy-going and mild-mannered. Most adults, one might even say, considered him polite. Except for possibly, Sheriff Draper, who was most likely biased, considering Blake had dated his daughter.

Despite this, Titusville had always been his home, and he had worked at his mother's diner, aptly named Linda's Diner, since he was fifteen years old. He had kept the same friends since he was four and was loyal to a fault.

It took a lot to ruffle Blake's feathers. On a Saturday night, when he went out drinking with his best friend, Dylan, and his brother, Jax, he never threw the first punch. He was just following their lead when the fighting broke out.

Snapping back to the situation, he realized that wasn't the point of his thought as Dylan greeted him, a fist pressed into his palm as he patted him on the back with his free hand.

What was the point he was trying to get to? Oh yes, Samantha Lancaster.

Despite his mild-mannered personality, he always found Samantha's presence enjoyable growing up. Sam was the complete opposite of mild-mannered. In fact, if he were to describe her, turbulent would be the first word that came to mind.

Yet, he always found that kind of endearing, in that *she's-your-best-friend's-little-sister-so-she's-definitely-off-limits* kind of way.

So, when he saw her standing at the hospital snack machine, promptly kicking the shit out of it, it was the first thing that had made him genuinely smile in weeks.

"How's Jax?" He watched the look of concern pass between the siblings and realized Jax's condition must be worse than he assumed.

"He's in surgery," Dylan said grimly. "Hey, did he say anything to you last night about heading out on Church Run?"

As Blake shook his head, he tried to remember the events of the evening prior. However, nothing stood out except for Jax leaving the bar to head back to their family's mechanic shop. "Not really," Blake said. "I thought he was going back to talk to your dad."

"Don't start, Dyl." Sam shook her head, and something passed between her and Dylan, a conversation that Blake didn't want to get involved in.

Trying to redirect the conversation, Blake looked at Sam. "So uh, long time no see. How long are you in town for?" It had been four years since he had seen the youngest Lancaster. It was the day she told him she got the job as a sports photographer for the Pittsburgh Pirates.

"Lost another one to the big city," he had teased her that evening over a cold beer at Boondocks.

While he wasn't jealous of the town's escapees, as he referred to them, he couldn't deny feeling a minor ache each time another one of them got out. Being a line cook at the diner gave him experience, but it wasn't the same as his dream of running a five-star restaurant.

Besides, there was no point in dwelling on it. There was no other option he would allow himself to consider, not even if the option was the best thing that had ever fallen in his lap. Blake wasn't allowed to dream because the diner wouldn't run itself. His mom and little sister, Kelley, needed him here.

But Sam leaving town had been a genuine loss for the Lancasters. Dylan never stopped talking about all the stuff his sister was up to in the city. And while Jax was more closed off and less talkative, he was quick to mention his sister's absence when events happened around town.

More than once or twice, they would dedicate a shot or two in her honor on a Saturday night. But if he was being honest, the town sucked without her spit fire, foul-mouthed, pain in the ass personality.

As his eyes devoured her body, the way her hips had a more delicate curve than the last time he saw her, or that he didn't remember how cute the dimple in her cheeks were when she smiled, he couldn't help but notice that she had matured since high school. Or perhaps his perspective had changed.

Either way, she looked damn good, though he wouldn't admit that to Dylan or her.

Maybe he felt that way because the only girls in town were the same ones that had been there since he was fourteen and he started noticing they had tits. *Small towns sucked.*

Suddenly realizing that Sam had been talking for about five minutes, and he hadn't heard a word she had said, Blake mentally scolded himself. He needed to stop staring at his best friend's little sister's tits and start listening instead.

"Anyway, I guess it will just depend on how much help Jax is going to need." Phew, he could at least figure out some of what he missed. At least he wouldn't come off like too much of a prick for asking a question and then tuning out on the answer.

"Well, if you need to eat, Mom's place is still the best food in town." He wasn't bragging. His food was good, and the safest bet if you didn't want to get salmonella from old man Rudy's bar down by the lake.

"I'll stop by to say hi," she said, gently rubbing his shoulder, picking up her bag of chips. "Thanks for buying the Funyuns. I haven't eaten all day," she said, stuffing a few into her mouth and mumbling, "I'm fucking starving."

Classic Sam.

"I have to get back to the diner. Kelley is incapable of being unsupervised for less than an hour without attempting to burn the place down." His sister was even more of a menace than Sam was when they were growing up. Despite recently graduating high school, he still didn't trust her alone in the diner. "Let me know how Jax is doing once he's out of surgery."

Dylan followed him to the exit; still upset about something he didn't want to discuss in front of his sister. "Are you sure he didn't say anything else last night?"

"Nothing. What's on your mind, Dyl?"

"It just doesn't make sense. Why was he up there?"

Dylan was always anxious about something. He supposed part of it might be from being a member of the "Dead Parent Club."

Dylan had lost his mom to cancer when he was only eight years old. He remembered back then thinking how awful it must feel to lose a parent. After the funeral, he came home and hugged both of his parents, feeling like a shit friend because he could still do that.

Then, a month before he turned sixteen, his mom got a phone call in the middle of the night. After that, he understood why Dylan felt so anxious all the time.

"Have you asked your dad?" It seemed like a logical question, but Dylan only stared at him, as if it was the first time he considered the question.

"Wouldn't he have just told me if Jax had talked to him last night?" His friend shrugged.

The doors to the hospital opened, and they walked outside toward the bike racks where his bike was sitting. "I don't know, man. You know how your dad has been for the last few months." He bent over and ticked the numbers into his combination lock, freeing his bicycle from the rack. "I have to get to work. I'll text you later, alright?"

"Yeah, see you later." Dylan stepped back into the hospital while Blake took off on his bike toward the diner.

As Blake rode through town, he passed Mrs. Baker's house, where she sat on her front porch swing. Waving at her, he anxiously hoped her dog wouldn't chase him down the street like it had last week.

Damn ankle biters.

Once he reached the park, he picked up speed and cut through the grass, hoping the shortcut would make up time. Approaching the diner, he turned onto Main Street, his bicycle wheels spinning rapidly.

Usually, he worked the day shift so his mom could get some rest. But with Jackson's accident, he had left Kelley in charge for a couple of hours. It gave him heartburn to think about what all Kelley was ignoring in his absence. While she took her job seriously, she wasn't as dedicated to the diner as he had been at eighteen.

As he approached the diner, the inviting glow of the neon sign came into view. The smell of the freshly brewed coffee carried through the air, mingling with his favorite smell of sizzling bacon. Thursday's special—Bacon double cheeseburger with fries for $10.

Sounds of laughter, quiet chatter, clinking dishes, and the diner's iconic eighties music drifted to him the moment he opened the front door. His sister was sitting at the counter, some slutty book open in front of her, bubble gum chomping in her mouth, as she teased her hair around her fingers. "It is a good thing I left you in charge," he said. She barely acknowledged his arrival, turning the page in her book and holding up a finger to keep him from interrupting her.

After finishing the page she was reading, she turned down the corner and closed the book. "I've got it all under control," she said, shaking her head at the couple in the corner booth. "Table Four has been here for an hour. I'm pretty sure he's just trying to get lucky."

Blake grabbed a clean cloth from under the counter and began cleaning up after the previous diners. "We're here to serve, Kels, not gossip."

"Whatever, he's gonna strike out, anyway," she said.

He glanced up at the couple without staring. They looked about his sister's age, and he had seen them around town a few times. He was fairly certain the guy's name was Joseph. "Yeah, and how do you know that?" he asked, his brow scrunched in confusion.

His sister laughed and leaned closer to him. "Because she doesn't play for the right team."

"Like the Mets?" he asked, trying to make sense of her comment.

"No, ya dumb twat," she snapped back.

"Language, Kels. If Mom hears you talking like that in here, she'll—" he started to say, but she interrupted him.

"Do what? Fire me? Twat, twat, twat," she taunted, as she picked up the dishcloth and threw it toward him.

"Cut it out."

"Anyway, she's a—you know, L word," his sister said, shrugging as if it was the most normal thing she had ever discovered. In any other town, maybe, but in their small town, it just wasn't something you shared. "Not even bi. I'm talking capital L."

He glanced back at the couple, noticing how the girl, whose name he was pretty sure started with an M, leaned away from Joseph. "How do you even know?" he asked, genuinely curious.

She snorted and picked up her book from the counter. "Because I made out with her last week behind the diner on my break. Duh!"

His sister loved reminding him of her bisexuality, which had driven him crazy growing up. Not only did he have to be on the lookout for random boys trying to get into his little sister's pants, but he also had to watch every single girl for ulterior motives too.

"Kels..." Just as he was about to address his sister, the door to the diner opened and his mother walked in. Kelley skipped toward her with an innocent smile, giving her a hug before she walked out the front door with a simple wave. Apparently, her shift was over.

"Hey Blake, did you make it to the hospital? How's Jackson?" His mother sat her purse behind the counter and checked the register. "I wanted to check on Ken but haven't had time today to do anything."

Ken, the Lancaster's father, was his mom's ex-boyfriend, and his dad's best friend from high school. All of that should be weird as shit, but in a small town, that was pretty common. "Didn't you get any rest this morning, Mom?" Concerned, he looked at his tired mother.

"I'm fine," she said. "Now tell me about Jackson. I'm just sick about it." He could see it on her face. Knew the reason she hadn't slept since last night when they got the news that Jackson had been in an accident.

It brought up too many memories. He knew she had spent all night reliving the nightmare.

We're sorry there has been an accident. Your husband didn't make it.

"He was in surgery when I got there. Dylan said he would text me when he's out." He put on his apron and grabbed the ticket for the next order. "Sam's back," he blurted. It wasn't like it should be a surprise anyway, not with Jax being in the hospital.

"Oh, how long has it been?" His mother's enthusiasm should have been a warning.

"Four years," he said with a shrug. "Give or take a few months."

"Is she staying long? Tell her to stop in." His mom greeted a customer as they walked in the front door.

"I did. She said she would."

"That's great. I wonder if she's dating anyone. She was always so adorable. I always thought the two of you would be perfect for each other."

He supposed he should have seen that coming. She had always favored Sam, but she had never really called it out. His mother had never been a fan of his ex-girlfriends, particularly his last one—Donna Draper, a fact she made abundantly clear. "Mom, stop," he pleaded with her. "She's Dylan's little sister."

"Everyone is someone's little sister, dear," she said.

He shook his head, his eyes scanning the kitchen. The old diner was showing its age, but cooking was the sole sanctuary that brought him joy. As he flipped over the burger, his mind wandered back to his mom's comments about Sam. Only his mother would try to uncomplicate the complicated. After all, if anyone understood complicated bullshit, it was his mother.

She had a long and messy history that intertwined and looped back on itself between his dad and Ken Lancaster.

However, fate intervened when a misunderstanding and a heated argument at prom led his mom to accept a ride home from Ken's best friend, Robert Forrester. The rest, as they say, was history.

Somehow, they all managed to remain friends, though Blake couldn't comprehend how.

But this situation was different. There was no way he would be able to un-fuck friendship. There was no point in entertaining thoughts of Sam Lancaster as anything more than Dylan's little sister. Not only would Dylan murder him, but Sam also lived in the city.

And Blake Forrester was never getting the hell out of Titusville.

Chapter Three

Samantha

Samantha ran her fingers along the wooden fireplace, leaving a trail of dust.

It had been years since she'd last been here, and now her family home felt unfamiliar, as if it belonged to someone else.

A sad exhale pushed past her lips before she brushed the grime from her hands. In need of a shower to wash away the day's exhaustion, she headed upstairs.

At least one thing remained unchanged: the shower's handle was still stuck, producing a scalding sprinkle rather than a warm spray.

Dammit, she missed the showerhead in her apartment.

The mirror steamed up quickly, and she wiped her hand across the glass to clear it. The person staring back at her was hardly recognizable compared to the person who had been here last. When she left home, she was twenty-two years old, and so unsure of herself. She had been so determined to leave Titusville and never look back.

Being in the city hadn't exactly been the exciting new adventure she had hoped it would be. Not that she didn't love her job. Photography had always been a part of her life. Even in high school, almost all the photos in the yearbook had taken by her. And being a sports photographer for the Pittsburgh Pirates was exciting and fun, but...

Sam undressed and stepped into the shower, determined to wash off the remains of the day without reminiscing about the sadder aspects of her life.

She soaped herself with a small washcloth, the cascading water flowing over her just as her mother's necklace snagged, emitting a quiet curse from her lips. She quickly grabbed the gold pendant, cautiously untangling it with her hand. Relief washed over her that no damage had been caused. The dragonfly pendant, the last thing her mother had ever given her before she died, was the only possession of hers that she truly cherished.

She finished her shower quicker than she was used to. Second-degree burns were too high a price to pay for shaving. It wasn't like anyone was going to be seeing her naked, anyway. A fact that was truly a damn shame.

When she finished drying her hair, the house was still quiet. She padded down the hall to her room, wrapped in a towel.

Her childhood bedroom still looked the same, with its dark, cool colors and forest green bedspread that paired well against the navy-blue curtains. Anyone who didn't know who had lived in this room would have assumed it belonged to one of her brothers.

Glancing at the pictures on her desk, Samantha smiled. One photo from a camping trip when she was sixteen caught her eye. Dylan and Blake were standing on either side of her, holding her up by her thighs, while Jax stood behind them with a grin on his face and bunny ears over her head.

Feeling nostalgic, she opened the drawer and rummaged inside the cramped space. Her fingers brushed against a small journal hidden in the back. A small smile curved her lips as she pulled it from its hiding place and ran her fingers over the leather binding. Samantha lay down on top of her comforter and released the strings, holding it closed.

Hidden within these pages were years of cherished memories. It became her solace after losing her mother—the one place where she could confide her deepest secrets. If only therapy were as affordable as stickers and glitter adorning the pages of a teenager's hopeful dreams.

As she flipped through the book, her attention was drawn to the inside of the front cover, which read: SL & BF 4EVER.

With a click of her tongue, her thoughts shifted to seeing Blake at the hospital. She couldn't help but wonder how he still looked so good. Couldn't he have gained weight or lost some hair? Did he really have to still look so attractive, like a piece of hunky eye-candy?

Just then, her phone buzzed on the nightstand, interrupting her nostalgic journey with a text from Dylan.

Dilly Bear

out of surgery

Dilly Bear

dads on his way

Sam

be right there

Dilly Bear

can you pick up food first?

Dilly Bear

Its bacon cheeseburger night at the diner

Sam

are you using me for food?

Dilly Bear

yes but you love me

Twenty minutes later, she found herself standing outside of Linda's Diner, relieved to see that the place hadn't changed at all. The familiar music of John Mellencamp playing just inside the doors brought a sense of comfort, knowing that at least some things remained the same.

As she pulled on the door handle, the bell jingled above her, signaling her entrance to the other diners. Mrs. Forrester's voice greeted her warmly. "There she is!"

"Hi, Mrs. F." She gladly embraced the woman's comforting presence, allowing herself to be enveloped in her arms.

"How's your brother?" she asked.

Gesturing toward the menu, she let out a sigh as she explained her brother's condition. "He just got out of surgery. My brother sent me here to pick up some food to take back to the hospital."

Mrs. Forrester invited her to sit down, stepping behind the counter to assist her. "Blake will take care of you, dear. Anything you need is on the house."

"Oh, that's unnecessary," she said, but her protest fell on deaf ears.

Through the window that separated the dining counter from the kitchen, Blake peered out from behind the heat lamps. Wiping away a bead of sweat with his elbow, he called out, "Oh, hey Sam! What can I get you?"

Well, hell, he still looked hot despite being sweaty and greasy from grilling all evening.

"Three specials, if that's not too much trouble." It was the small smirk that left her feeling hot all over. She was here for Jax's accident, she reminded herself, not some unrequited high school fantasy.

"Is Jax out of surgery?" he asked.

"Yeah, I'm actually taking this over to the hospital now," she said, her voice blending with the melodic rhythm of the song playing in the background. Leaning against the cold, smooth counter, she tapped her fingers to the beat of "What's Love Got to Do with It," feeling the faint vibrations of the music reverberating through her fingertips.

"How's Pittsburgh?" Mrs. Forrester sat down on the stool next to her, trying to engage in conversation.

Sam shrugged, feeling unsure about how to answer without sounding dissatisfied with her life away from town. She wasn't unhappy, but sometimes she wondered if there was something missing. She didn't exactly have friends back in Pittsburgh. She had acquaintances at best, people she could maybe grab a beer with, but friends? Those were few and far between. City life was pretty lonely, if she was being honest with herself. And right now, it wasn't the time for honesty. "They keep me busy. I'm always on the run, you know. But overall, it's great. Really great," Sam said, trying to put a positive spin on her answer.

"We miss you around here," Mrs. Forrester said, glancing up at her son. "I swear Dylan and Blake could use a bit of your guidance sometimes."

Blake's voice carried loudly from the kitchen, interrupting their conversation. "Mom!"

"Alright, alright," Mrs. Forrester said, standing up and pressing her hand along her arm. Leaning over, she whispered in Sam's ear, "Boys will be boys, you know."

Blake entered the dining room from the swinging steel door, carrying a bag of food. "Here you go. I even added some extra fries for Dylan. He always eats more than one order," he said, handing the bag to Sam.

"Thanks again. I really appreciate it. I got you next time," Sam said, knowing that she would be back again before she left town.

"Blake, you should go with her," Mrs. Forrester suddenly suggested, surprising both Sam and Blake.

"What?" Blake said loudly, caught off guard by his mother's suggestion.

"She needs help to carry all that food, and Dylan could use your help too," his mother said, her eyes conveying a look of finality.

"You don't have to, Blake. I can manage," Sam said, not wanting to impose on him.

"Nah, can you just give me a minute to go change? I don't want to smell like grease all night," Blake said, untying his apron from behind his back.

"Sure, I'll meet you in the car. I'm just going to take the food out there," Sam said, hopping down off the stool and tucking the food under her arm.

"Great. Well, this worked out splendidly," Mrs. Forrester said with a self-satisfied expression. She embraced Sam before gently ushering her out the door, leaving Sam alone with the dreadful realization that she was about to be alone in a car with Blake.

She barely had time to think about what she was going to say to him when the sound of nails on a chalkboard hit her ears. "Is that Samantha Lancaster I see, or do my eyes deceive me?" Nostalgia swept over her like a heavy blanket, making her feel small and vulnerable. It was as if she was suddenly back in high school, in that damp locker room, reeking of teenage insecurity and self-doubt. She could already feel her examining her unkempt curls, the weight of the girl's judgmental eyes upon her, dissecting her every flaw and imperfection.

"Donna Draper, imagine running into you." Not like it was that hard. It was inevitable that in such a small town, she would eventually run into people she knew here. She had just hoped she wouldn't be here long enough to run into her.

"I'm surprised to see you here. I thought you were too good for Titusville after you abandoned your family."

Sam's laughter erupted into a loud snorting sound that she couldn't control. "Shame, I always hoped therapy might be a good self-help option for you."

"Oh, honey, I'm a delight. Everyone knows it. Just ask your brothers or any of my 958,000 Instagram followers."

Samantha fought the urge to roll her eyes. If fortune was measured by Instagram followers, Donna Draper would be Jeff Bezos rich by now. Thankfully, life didn't work that way.

"Honestly, my brothers are a little busy right now, Donna." She yanked the door of her VW bug open and placed the bags of food on the floor of the backseat, slamming it closed behind her.

"Aww, are your brothers too busy for their long-forgotten sister?"

She really didn't have time for this stupid bitch. "Honestly, I don't have time for whatever this is, Donna," she snapped, her patience wearing thin like a fraying rope.

"Whatever." Donna headed toward the diner door just as it opened. She paused, her eyes meeting Blake's in surprise. Blake's gaze shifted between Donna and Samantha, his expression revealing a hint of concern. "Blake, hey, I was just coming for the Thursday night special."

Blake's smile was friendly, but his mannerism toward Donna was curt and formal. "Oh, well, Sam and I were just leaving. But feel free to head inside."

She hid the growing smirk on her face as Blake pushed past an exasperated Donna and walked toward her. Suddenly she felt like she was in one of those eighties films, like *Pretty in Pink*, where the weirdly unattractive girl, played by an actually attractive actress, won the heart of the hot guy at the end of the film and everyone cheered.

Maybe *Pretty in Pink* was a poor example, she thought, because honestly, as far as love interests went, Blaine sucked. Justice for Duckie.

Blake was standing in front of her, and she realized she must have been standing there thinking about the movie and not paying attention because now he was staring down at her with that adorable, goofy grin on his face, and she had no idea what he was saying.

"Shit, fuck." She shook her head, her palm resting against her forehead. Her face felt warm. She was sure she had turned a light shade of pink. "Sorry, I zoned out."

"Do that often? Just randomly spew curse words and then zone out?!" Blake's question hung in the air, causing her cheeks to flush an even deeper shade of red. She tried to conceal the embarrassment that was threatening to consume her, but it only made it worse.

She let out a nervous laugh. "Just tired, I guess." She shuddered, his touch sending a wave of goosebumps across her skin as his hand caressed her arm and shoulder.

"You've had a hectic day. And I'm sure it wasn't easy getting the call about Jax." His vulnerable eyes, filled with understanding, made her feel guilty about accepting his comfort, considering his past.

"I'm sure that Dylan's wasn't exactly easy for you either." She noticed him blink and shift his weight awkwardly. He glanced down at his feet, kicking at the rocks next to the pavement with the tip of his shoe.

"Yeah, uh," he said, running his hand through his messy hair. She swallowed, unable to ignore how it fell around his forehead. She may have spent years getting over her crush on Blake, but it only took seconds to be reminded of how adorable he was when he was awkward or nervous. "We should leave," he said.

"Sure," she said. He pushed a hand into his pocket and stepped around her to open the passenger side door.

She refrained from laughing as she watched him squeeze his large body into her compact car. In the past, she had fantasized about making out with him in her car, but now, seeing him uncomfortably squeezed into the front seat, she doubted if those scenarios were even feasible. Still, she thought it might be worth trying a few, purely for scientific purposes.

The moment she closed the door; a cloak of darkness enveloped them. She turned the engine on, and the car sputtered to life. "I can't believe this thing is still running," he said with a boyish smile that sent her stomach into a somersault.

"Hey, don't make fun of her. She gets the job done," she said, patting her hand on the steering wheel. The car held a special place in her heart because it had belonged to her mother.

He held his hands in front of him defensively. "Trust me, I am the last person to give anyone shit about what they drive. In fact, I still ride a Schwinn everywhere I go."

"What happened to the GT?" she asked, noticing that for the second time that night, she had made him uncomfortable again.

Way to freaking go, Sam.

"It's a small town, not like I need to get anywhere fast," he said with a shrug, giving her a bullshit answer. But she wasn't going to press him any further.

"So, uh, how's Pittsburgh?" he asked, seeming to stare at her intently. "And not that fake ass answer you gave my mom." He crinkled his nose, mocking her in a high-pitched voice. "It's great, really great. The greatest great you can great."

She opened her mouth to respond, then shut it. How did he see through her so easily? "Pittsburgh is fine. I have a great job, and I enjoy living in the city."

"So then, what was with the sad eyes and melancholy tone? And don't deny it. I've known you for far too long, Sam," he said, challenging her.

She laughed, her head shaking gently. "Do you ever wonder if this is all there is to life?" she asked, realizing it wasn't a question she had intended to ask. But now that the words were out there, they seemed to have a life of their own. "It's like I finally escaped this place, doing what I love in the city, where I can enjoy a slice of pizza and a beer at three in the morning if I feel like it. Yet, sometimes, I can't help but feel like there's something missing."

"I think the point to that would be heartburn," he said with a small laugh, causing her to turn toward him. He shrugged. "Pizza at 3:00 AM. As for the meaning of life," he confessed, "you're on your own there. I don't have a damn clue about any of that."

After parking her car in front of the hospital, she turned to face him. "Did you ever think about leaving Titusville?"

He reached into the backseat and grabbed the bags of food from the floor. "It's not like I have that option. Mom and Kelley need me here." His reply gave her a sense that there was more behind it.

"But if you had the opportunity, would you have wanted to?" she asked.

He exhaled loudly and bit his lip before speaking. "You swear never to repeat this." With an intense gaze, his brown eyes piercing hers, he added, "Not even to Dylan."

She nodded enthusiastically. "Of course, I won't say a word."

"Sam, I'm serious. This can't get out. I'm only telling you because, well—you're going back to Pittsburgh and won't be here to spill my secrets, and honestly, I've been dying to tell someone for months about this."

Suddenly, she felt incredibly special, as if she was being invited into an elite club. The Blake Forrester secret keeper club, population of two. Sixteen-year-old Samantha Lancaster could eat her heart out.

"I got accepted into the Culinary Institute of America," he said, his eyes glimmering with excitement and pride. After a moment of reflection, he let out a sigh and continued with a joyful expression. "It felt incredible to finally say those words out loud to someone."

"Blake, that's incredible. Why haven't you told anyone else?" she asked, her mind overflowing with questions.

"It's in New York. I can't just leave all the responsibility of the diner on Mom and run off to the city," he said.

"But it's a once-in-a-lifetime opportunity. I'm sure your mom would understand."

He pulled on the handle and shoved his door open. "We can't all be lucky like you, Sam." The words caused her to flinch, but before she could respond, he had slammed the door shut, leaving her alone in silence.

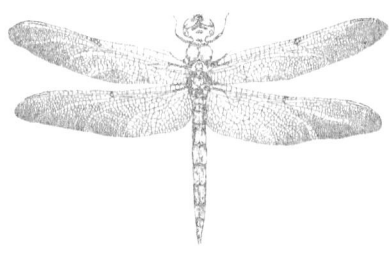

Chapter Four

Blake

B lake sat in a chair in the hallway while Sam and her family talked to the Doctor inside Jackson's room. He couldn't hear everything, but he noticed a raised voice, which was presumably Dylan or his dad.

Based on the information he was gathering from the conversation, Jax's surgery had gone well. However, he had not yet woken up. The worst part, as he had heard, was that it was going to take at least four to six weeks before Jax could leave the hospital. There would be an additional six weeks, or possibly even longer, of physical therapy before he could regain his ability to walk around like normal. That was sure to piss him off, he imagined, knowing Jax the way he did.

He wasn't sure how they were going to handle the shop without Jax's assistance. Although Dylan helped with oil changes and the occasional simple brake job now and then, it was Jax who knew how to do the more complicated repairs. It was Jax who did most of the heavy lifting with the customers.

Dylan may be his best friend, but he couldn't exactly make excuses for him, especially considering Dylan's subpar customer service skills. In fact, if they relied on him alone, the business would most likely go under in a month. While Ken Lancaster owned the shop, it was Jax who single-handedly kept Lancaster's Auto Repair afloat.

Suddenly, the sound of approaching footsteps sounded on the other side of the door as Dylan and Samantha burst in, their voices raised. "I can handle it," Dylan said, arguing with his sister.

"You're going to take over the store *and* play nursemaid to Jax?" It wasn't a question. "And you think that won't be more stress on Dad?"

In an attempt to go unnoticed, Blake stood up and took a few quiet steps toward the hall. "Blake, tell her," Dylan said, pulling him into the conversation. "Tell her I can manage the shop and help with Jax." Sam turned to Blake, waiting for his input. Blake stared at her, struggling to find the right words that wouldn't put him on his best friend's shit list.

"Dylan, I understand your desire to help both Dad and Jax, but it's simply too much for one person, and you shouldn't have to shoulder all of that responsibility alone." Sam said, turning toward Blake. "Help me out here. He can't do it all, and you know that better than anyone."

Blake stared at the two siblings, feeling helpless. "I—um, well, she has a point, Dylan," he said, hesitantly interjecting himself into the conversation.

"Are you kidding me? You're going to take her side. *My* best friend," Dylan said, his voice filled with frustration.

"Would you stop acting like an idiot and just listen to her? I don't even know what's going on, but if she's offering to help you, just take the damn support," Blake said, trying to get his friend to understand he wasn't taking sides.

Sam smiled graciously at him. "Thank you, Blake."

Dylan frowned, shifting his focus back toward her. "I can't ask you to jeopardize your job, Sam. Three months away from the city is a long time. You barely even come home for Christmas. And that's when there isn't a crisis back here to deal with."

"And you always complain that I don't come home enough. At least this way I can be here for the holidays and take care of Jax. Plus, I can sniff around and see if there really is something going on with Dad," Sam said, watching Dylan's reaction intently.

She really was brilliant. Sam was playing into his own conspiracy theories now, and he had to give her credit. Growing up, Sam had always been a formidable force in arguments. She was also clever in dealing with her brothers, always knowing which levers to pull. Offering Dylan an ally in helping to confirm his anxiety-driven suspicions behind the accident was a smart play on Sam's part. Besides, if Jax was really going to be laid up for three months, there was no way Dylan and his dad could do this on their own.

"What about your job? Three months is a long time for you to pack up and leave the city." Dylan raised a valid concern, and Blake couldn't help but turn back to Sam to look for her reaction as if watching some tennis match being played in one of those cheesy soap operas his mom and sister liked to watch.

"Lucky for you, the Pirates' crappy play and inability to make the playoffs this year benefits you. The team doesn't report for spring training in Florida until next year in February," Sam said, pointing out a pretty valid point. "So, I'm sure if I call and tell them the situation, they'll understand."

"What's Casey gonna say about it?" Dylan asked.

A fire burned in Sam's eyes for a short moment before she responded, "I don't see how this would be any of his business."

"Are you sure he's aware of that?" Dylan's voice was sharp and accusatory, indicating that he clearly wasn't a fan of Casey. Blake had no clue who Casey was, but if his best friend wasn't a fan, perhaps there was a reason not to like him.

"Casey is none of *your* business, Dylan," Sam said. This soap opera was getting more interesting by the minute.

Dylan pouted silently, while Sam stood with her arms crossed tightly against her chest, clearly displeased. The three of them remained in silence, leaving Blake curious about the cause of their tension. He wondered who this Casey guy was and what had transpired between them.

However, before he could inquire, Mr. Lancaster appeared in the hallway with news that caused everyone to react. "He's awake."

Blake followed Sam and Dylan into the room, where everyone rushed to Jax's bedside. Jax's weak eyes stared back at them as he finally spoke with a hoarse voice, "Did I miss a party?"

Sam stepped up to his bedside, grabbed his hand, and expressed her worry in a way that only Sam could. "You son of a bitch. Don't you ever scare me like that again."

"How bad is the bike?" He coughed, looking around the room as everyone stared at him.

Dylan chuckled. "Afraid you're gonna have a lot of work to do to fix that piece of junk. I think parts of it are still stuck in the tree up on Church Run."

"Shit." Jax stared at the light over his bed.

"All that matters is that you're still with us, kid." Mr. Lancaster's voice sounded small and distant as he stood at the back of the room.

Which made Blake himself question why exactly he was so far away from his son? Dylan and Sam exchanged glances, mirroring Blake's thoughts about Mr. Lancaster's distance from his son. It struck Blake as odd that Mr. Lancaster hadn't even approached the bed or shown any signs of comfort since Jax had woken up.

Blake had always known Mr. Lancaster to be a bit of a hands-off type of dad when raising his kids. *"Emotions are a luxury, not a requirement,"* he used to tell Dylan.

It was a stark contrast to Blake's own upbringing, where his mom had encouraged embracing and understanding emotions. Blake couldn't help but wonder how his mom and Mr. Lancaster had remained close despite their differences, especially with their shared romantic history. But at the core of it all, they couldn't be more complete opposite as human beings.

Jax seemed to regard his father's words without comment, instead looking back at his siblings and smiling fondly at his sister. "I'm sorry I made you drive all the way down here."

"Nonsense. It's my job to take care of my idiot brothers when they do stupid shit, right?" she said, holding her hand over her mouth to disguise her comical cough.

Dylan playfully kicked her foot from behind. "Tell her to go home, Jax. She's threatening to stay for three months and take care of you."

She quickly scolded her brother, "Tattletale," before turning her attention back to Jax. "It's either you let me do it, or you're stuck with Dylan as your bedside nurse. Your choice, bro."

Jax shook his head, and Blake could see the reality sinking in for him. "Woah, I don't need no bedside nurse," he said with a low painful groan, attempting to sit up in the bed. "Just get me out of this bed and get me some crutches or something."

Dylan and Sam exchanged concerned glances. Finally, Dylan relented. "It's not that easy, Jax. They won't release you for another four weeks at least. And then you'll need time for physical therapy before you can walk again."

"Fuck that." Jax's angry voice echoed through the room, the beeping of the hospital machines serving as the only other sound.

Sam let out a sigh and looked over at her dad, as if seeking his support, but her dad only retreated further into the corner. She seemed to realize she was on her own here as she turned back to her brother. "Jax, your accident was serious. You can't just walk out of here."

Jax defiantly responded, "You ever see anyone tell me I can't do something, sis? Fuck the Doc. Fuck this shit. Fuck all this 'woe is Jax' diagnosis that I keep hearing from both of you. I'm getting out of here." He forcefully tugged on his sheets, exposing himself to the room.

Did he really need a reminder of why everyone called Jax 'Big Dick' Lancaster in high school?

Sam and Dylan attempted to restrain him while Blake stepped forward. However, the moment Jax's feet hit the tile floor, he collapsed in pain. Sam glanced back at Blake, exhaustion and irritation evident in her eyes. "Can you go get the nurse?"

He nodded, trying to convey an apology for the situation Sam was enduring. He didn't even know what he was apologizing for. Jax wasn't his brother. Nevertheless, she was only trying to help, and it seemed like both of her brothers were making things more difficult for her. He turned and hurried out of the room, heading toward the nurses' station to seek assistance.

There certainly was never a dull moment with the Lancaster family, but he had to admit Sam's return had made things a lot more interesting around here.

Chapter Five

Samantha

S am had spent the last two days driving back to Pittsburgh to pack up some of her belongings, and then returning home to get settled into her old room in her family home. Fortunately, her boss was completely understanding of her situation and offered her the time off from work that she needed to take care of her family.

It was a relief, not a moment too soon. After watching her father with Jax at the hospital, she thought maybe Dylan wasn't imagining this conspiracy between the two of them. There was something strange between her brother and her father, and she couldn't explain her father's distant behavior. While Jax seemed aggravated about his condition, she couldn't help but feel that there was more to it.

As she pulled her hair up into a messy bun on top of her head, her phone buzzed on her nightstand across the room. Initially, she was half tempted to ignore it, desperate to go for a walk before she was due to be at the hospital to check on Jax.

However, she tapped on the screen, just to make sure it wasn't something important, and groaned immediately.

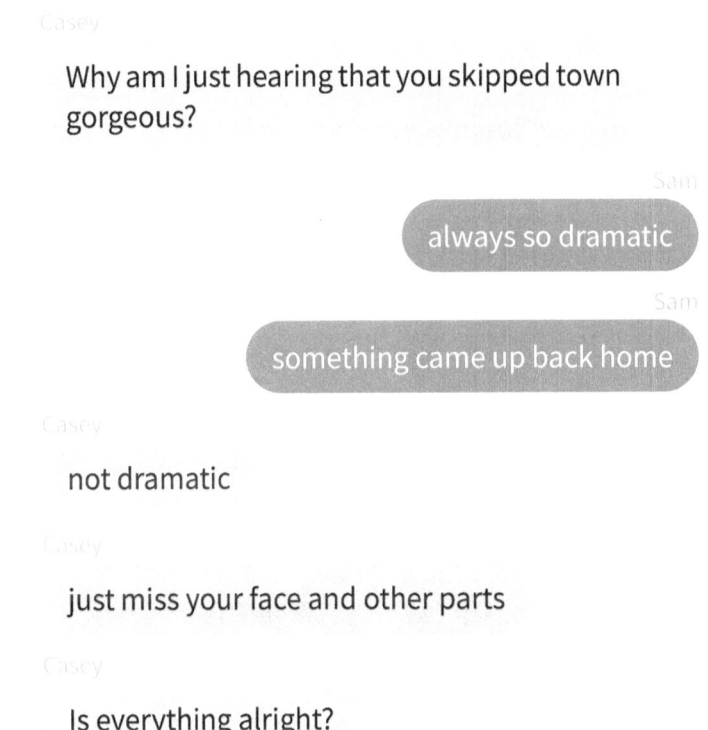

Casey

Why am I just hearing that you skipped town gorgeous?

Sam

always so dramatic

Sam

something came up back home

Casey

not dramatic

Casey

just miss your face and other parts

Casey

Is everything alright?

She couldn't help but groan deeply as she read her messages from Casey; he was one of those habits that seemed impossible to quit. Deep down, she knew he wasn't the right fit for her. Despite his reputation as a ladies' man, with his dirty blond hair, stunning blue eyes, and an attractive physique that could inspire one of those spicy novels all the girls were reading these days, she knew better.

As the pitcher for the Pittsburgh Pirates, he exuded confidence and was well aware of his appeal; they didn't call him Casanova for nothing around the locker room.

However, he was also a grade-A asshole, or so Sam thought most of the time. Casey was the easiest friends with benefits she had ever had. They never truly graduated to dating, yet every time she tried to cut things off with him completely, she fell back into his bed. But hey, you can't blame a girl for wanting some action now and then, right?

Sam
my brother had an accident

Sam
gonna need to stay in town for a few months to help him recover

Casey
Shit! sounds serious! do you need help?

Sam
No, im good. thanks for the offer.

Casey
text if you need anything

Casey
even if its just a dick pic

Oh, for heaven's sake, she thought. Only Casey would think a dick pic was a legitimate offer of help. She tossed her phone onto the bed and finished getting ready.

Standing at the entrance to the trailhead, Sam took a deep breath and stretched her legs, eager to embark on the familiar trails she hadn't walked in years. For Sam, walking had always been a way to relieve stress, a sanctuary where she could escape from the world. As she glanced at Jax's dog, Whiskey, an excitable Shepard-Great Dane mix Jax had raised since he was a puppy, bouncing happily beside her, she knew these trails would become a regular destination for her over the next three months. "Alright, boy, let's go."

With each step, the fresh scent of oak filled Sam's nostrils, while tall trees lined the trail, their leaves rustling in the gentle breeze. A sense of familiarity washed over her, as she had fallen in love with these trails during her childhood. The rhythmic sound of her feet hitting the dirt path echoed in her ears as she followed the route she used to have memorized. Whiskey bounded ahead, his infectious energy making Sam wonder if he, too, knew her secret spot.

The trail opened up to a breathtaking clearing under the tree's canopy. A crystal-clear stream that looked almost ethereal, its gentle babble a comforting soundtrack to the serene scene. She sat on the mossy rock, feeling the coolness seep through her yoga tights. Whiskey, ever the explorer, dipped his paws into the stream, splashing water playfully around him.

"Hey, be careful," she said, her tone firm, as she realized how wet the pup was getting, bouncing in and out of the water, his fur dripping. "You're going to make a mess of my car."

Startled by the sound of squealing tires behind her, she watched as Whiskey ran off toward the noise. "Whiskey, get back here," she called out.

Blake's voice startled her. "Woah, hey boy, what are you doing out here?" he said, swiftly dismounting his bike and running his fingers through the dog's mane. Their eyes met. "Hey, Sam, it's been ages since I last saw someone up here."

"Not much has changed," she said. Her eyes scanned the canopy covered creek, remembering all the times she had taken solace in this hiding place growing up. She stood up and tossed a stick across the creek, prompting Whiskey to eagerly chase after it.

She sensed his eyes fixed on her, causing her to fidget nervously on her feet. She couldn't understand why his mere presence made her stomach flutter. After all, she was no longer the same schoolgirl who engraved their initials on a tree when she was sixteen. Ironically, that very tree stood hidden from sight, just ten feet away from them.

"How's Jax?"

She shrugged. "Just as cranky as ever, honestly." She returned to her seat on the rock. She watched Whiskey playing in the creek. Blake walked over and sat beside her, kicking a few rocks and rustling leaves under his feet.

His deep laugh put her at ease. "Sounds like Jax. I'm sure he's going stir crazy being trapped in a bed," he said, pausing as if he was remembering something. His hand gently caressed the back of his neck. Sam couldn't help but let her eyes wander.

This place may not have changed, but Blake had matured in all the right ways. His body seemed different, more defined. His once chubby cheeks had given way to a more sculpted jawline, evidence of his physical maturity. Although not as muscular as her brother Jackson, Blake's features were more subtle, evident in the way his biceps curved, straining against the fabric of his sleeves. Sam's mind wandered, envisioning all the possibilities of what those powerful arms could do to her.

"I don't think I've ever seen Jax off his feet for more than a day," he said with a snort, "and that was because he was piss ass drunk and fell into the lake in the middle of January. I swear he almost caught his death."

Samantha blinked, still distracted by her exploration of Blake's body. The absent-minded laugh she let out felt ridiculous to her, reminding her of the foolish feelings she used to experience during high school when she found herself alone with him. She mentally slapped herself. After all, she was a sexually active twenty-six-year-old now, and she was behaving as if she was twelve-year-old, just discovering that boys had penises.

Pull yourself together, Sam!

Whiskey trotted over, his tail thumping a happy rhythm against the ground, and dropped his creek-soaked face onto her lap. With a small squeal of surprise caused by the sudden cold, she instinctively patted his head. "I think he misses Jax."

As Blake stared out at the creek, his jaw tight, he only hummed in response. She tried not to get too distracted by him, but then she heard him speak unexpectedly. "Who's Casey?"

It was not what she had expected him to ask. She stuttered, "Um, sorry, what?"

"Casey, you and Dylan were fighting about him at the hospital. Who is he?" He turned to look at her, his face a mask of emotion.

Surprised that he remembered their conversation from the first night, she tightly gripped Whiskey's fur and answered, "Casey Anderson, he's a pitcher for the Pirates."

Understanding her words, Blake nodded. "Number twenty-four, right? He got moved up last year."

Taking a deep breath to gather her thoughts, she nodded. "That's the one."

"Boyfriend?" Whether Casey was her boyfriend, coming from Blake Forrester of all people, was the last conversation she expected to have with him.

"I think I would use the term boyfriend very loosely. We've never even dated, really," she said.

Sarcasm laced Blake's words as he noted, "Dylan seems fond of him."

Unable to contain herself, she snorted at his comment. "Yeah, well, you know Dylan. He still pretends I'm a virgin who doesn't know the word blowjob."

Caught off guard, Blake choked, cursing under his breath as he struggled to breathe. Trying to offer comfort, she patted him on the back while enjoying the humor of the situation.

"Besides, Casey isn't exactly boyfriend material. Unless you consider how much he loves himself," she said, pursing her lips. "It's the curse of being around ball players day in and day out. Half of them want to screw you and the other half want you to screw their friends. But all of them want you to take their picture on game day so they get the best coverage possible in the press."

"That doesn't sound like the Sam I remember," he said, his eyes widening in shock and his eyebrows furrowing in disbelief. The sound of his voice carried a mix of surprise and disapproval that shocked her.

"Excuse you, Blake," she said, as the irritation bubbled inside her. Her eyes narrowed and her lips tightened, revealing her displeasure. "I am a professional," she said. "Casey is the only baseball player I have slept with on the team."

Blake grunted his continued judgement as her lips parted further in annoyance.

"You know, most of them are ridiculously flirty," she continued, her voice now filled with a touch of bitterness, "but I moved to the city for my career, not to play mommy to a bunch of baseball babies." Her words hung in the air, crossing her arms with all the determination she could muster. "However, if I did, that would be my choice," she said, her voice now strong and assertive. "If I were a man, no one would bat an eye if I slept my way through the team. And don't you dare pretend that Dylan keeps it in his pants?"

He raised his hands in a defensive gesture, his palms facing her. At least his voice carried an air of reassurance and apology. "Hey, hey, I wasn't judging you," he pleaded. "You have every right to whore yourself out to whoever you want," he said sarcastically.

"Damn straight I do," she responded. "Not that I'm a whore, mind you," she quickly clarified.

"Of course not," he murmured, with a smirk.

Sam chuckled, trying to ease the tension. "Well, now that we've settled that." She looked back toward his bike. "Tell me why you're riding that thing around, and not that sexy ass GT Mustang?" She turned back and looked him in the eye. "And don't make up some excuse. You owe me that much after just calling me a whore."

He winced and pulled at the collar of his shirt. "To be clear, I never actually called you a whore, Sam."

"Tomato, Tomahto, Blake! Answer the question."

"I guess I just don't want to drive it," he said hesitantly. Sam noticed a hint of sadness in his eyes, as if there was a weight on his shoulders. However, she also thought the answer was a copout, which caused her to let out a soft chuckle.

Bewildered by her reaction, he looked at her. "You don't want to drive a sexy ass sports car?" she asked, a mischievous glint in her eyes. "Afraid you'll end up having too much sex because of it? Were you going for some kind of Forrest Gump vibe with the bike?"

Irritation flashed across his face, forming a faint frown on his brow. "Look, after Dad died, I just didn't see the point in driving it, okay!" he said, his tone laced with an emotion that shocked her.

A jolt of surprise from his unexpected outburst heightened her senses. She knew the car held sentimental value, as it was a gift from his father before his passing. However, it was still a goddamn good-looking car. "Alright, I still don't get it, Blake," she said, softening her voice.

His posture shifted, his body tensing up as if ready to defend himself. "He was supposed to teach me to drive in it, and then he died," he said, his expression filled with a mix of grief and frustration.

Sam gently asked, "So you don't know how to drive?"

His frustration bubbled over. "Of course, I know how to drive. I'm twenty-eight years old, Sam. I'm not an idiot."

Sam shrugged, accepting his response. "Then I still don't get it."

A mix of anger and desperation simmered beneath the surface. "I just don't want to drive his damn car, alright," he muttered.

Sam realized that driving the car held a deeper significance for him, a reminder of a loss that couldn't be undone. She knew that better than anyone, as she reached up and touched the dragonfly necklace hanging from her neck, a constant reminder of her mother. "Driving that car changes nothing, you know that, right? Even if you drive it, your dad will still be gone. Sometimes a car is just a car," she said gently, her words hanging in the air.

"Jesus Christ, Sam," he murmured, responding with anguish and frustration. "I know you mean well, but sometimes you really should keep your thoughts inside your head."

He snatched up his bike and took off down the path before she could react, leaving her alone with her thoughts.

Samantha dangled her feet from her dad's shop counter as her brother tinkered with a Chevy Subaru engine. The energetic sound of Fall Out Boy blared from the stereo in the corner, creating a lively atmosphere. Meanwhile, her dad had been pacing in his office, engrossed in a phone call for the past twenty minutes.

Absentmindedly, she dug into the countertop with a screwdriver in her hand, lost in her thoughts about Blake. It had been three days since their last conversation, and she couldn't shake the feeling that she owed him an apology.

Growing up, Samantha's upbringing had taught her not to let emotions control her. Death was a part of life, and it didn't dictate one's choices. However, she realized Blake was different. He struggled with his father's death, and the Forrester family openly mourned for months after his car accident.

Reflecting on this, Sam recognized that she may have been too curt with Blake, despite her reputation for being blunt and direct about everything.

"Earth to Sam!" Dylan's raised voice interrupted her thoughts, causing her to drop the screwdriver.

"Sorry, what?" she said, startled.

"Can you grab that wrench for me?" Dylan, his face smeared with grease and dirt, emerged from beneath the lifted Subaru.

She hopped off the counter and retrieved the wrench for him. "Have you seen Blake lately?"

Dylan wrinkled his nose and narrowed his eyes, staring back at her. "Blake? Yeah, why?"

"Oh, I just wanted to thank him," Sam said, trying to come up with a reason. "You know, for the food the other night."

Dylan's response carried a hint of sarcasm. "Pretty sure that's his job."

Sam chuckled. Dylan had a point. "Yeah, right! Of course." She laughed as Dylan disappeared back under the vehicle, slapping her forehead in amusement. It was clear that she wouldn't get any information about Blake from Dylan without him asking more questions.

No, if she wanted to find out how Blake was doing after their conversation, she needed to gather the courage to go find out for herself.

"I've got to go to Erie," their dad suddenly announced from behind them.

Dylan emerged from the vehicle. "What for? I thought you were going to help with the four oil changes I still have to do today."

Their dad replied with a frown, "It can't be helped, kiddo. I'll be back by dinner." He quickly hugged her and brushed a kiss against her forehead before hurrying out of the open garage toward his beat-up truck.

She frowned at Dylan, perplexed by the exchange. "What was that all about? What's in Erie?"

Dylan shrugged. "Shit, if I know. I told you something was going on with him." Reluctantly, she agreed with her brother, knowing he was right. Maybe she would ask Jax about it the next time she was at the hospital, if it didn't piss him off too much. "You sure you don't want to learn how to do oil changes?" Dylan asked, shooting her a sheepish grin.

"Sorry, brother, but I have plans to wash my hair," she said, blowing him a kiss. Hurrying out the door, she followed the same path her father had taken, paying no attention to her brother's expletive curses from the garage behind her.

Chapter Six

Blake

The diner was filled with the aroma of sizzling bacon as Blake expertly flipped pancakes for the breakfast rush. Each flip was perfectly timed to the rhythmic beat of "Uptown Girl" blasting from the speakers. It had been three days since he had spoken to Sam on the trail. During the first two days, he sulked like a child over her brash comment, even though he had always known that Sam was straightforward, but her words had still stung.

However, when he woke up this morning, he realized he was behaving like a dumbass. He knew Sam wouldn't intentionally say something to hurt him—yet she had. Losing his father had been a significant event in his life, one that had influenced every subsequent experience after he turned sixteen. But being mad at Sam about it wasn't going to change it.

As he was lost in his thoughts, the smell of burning pancakes yanked him back to reality. He scraped off the burned food and started a new batch, muttering a string of curse words.

"Distracted much, loser?" His sister Kelley stood at the window, impatiently waiting for her ticket. "Table Three is still waiting on those pancakes," she said sarcastically.

Annoyed, Blake snapped, "I know, alright? I'm working on it." He needed to pull himself together and focus on his job. However, he couldn't help but question what was happening to him. Yes, Sam's words had sparked anger within him, but it was the fact that he couldn't stop thinking about her that truly frustrated him.

His sister cast a disdainful glance and scoffed. "You're in a real shithole mood!"

Irritated, he snapped back, "Watch your language, Kels!" The bell over the diner jingled as the subject of all his thoughts walked in.

Kelley rushed forward squealing, "Oh my God, Sam!" She enveloped Sam in a warm hug.

As they embraced, he watched the exchange between Sam and his sister. "How did you get so big?" Sam teasingly examined her. "The last time I saw you, I swear you were five inches shorter and still rocking those adorable pigtails."

Chuckling, Kelley responded exactly how he expected his sister to. "Don't knock it, girl, pigtails can still be sexy."

Blake groaned. *Heavens, his sister was a menace.*

"Don't I know that?" Sam's flirty tone caused the comment to lose its benign and innocent nature. Suddenly, an image of Sam in pigtails and her little white tank top flooded his mind, and he cursed himself for even entertaining such thoughts.

What was he even doing? he thought. It was Samantha Lancaster, his best friend's little sister.

Smacking his hand on the bell in front of him, he signaled to his sister that the pancakes for Table Three were ready. The noise echoed through the diner, catching Sam's attention. Their eyes met at that moment. "Hey, Sam," he greeted her, and she nodded in his direction.

He kept his eye on her as she spent the next few hours in a corner booth, enjoying toast and jam with a diet soda, engrossed in reading her book, *The Catcher in the Rye.*

"You should probably just take a break and go talk to her instead of staring at her like a stalker," his sister said, causing his head to snap in her direction.

"What?" he asked, surprised.

"Go talk to Sam," she said firmly. "Clearly you want to. You've been staring at her for two hours already!"

"I have not." He stared down at his apron, absentmindedly picking at random bits of food stuck to the fabric. "I've just been judging her taste in breakfast choices."

Eyeing him with exasperation, she shrugged. "Whatever loser, no balls," she said before walking away with a flick of her hair.

He stared after her, leaning against the doorway to the kitchen. Maybe she was right. After all, Sam had been at the diner for hours, wasting time for a reason. Perhaps she wanted to talk to him as well.

He pulled his apron over his head and walked toward the corner booth, smoothly sliding into the seat across from her. As he sat down, he placed a fresh glass of diet soda on the table. "Is this really what you eat for breakfast?"

Startled, she looked up at him, closed her book, and smiled. "Usually, it's fruit loops, but unfortunately, I'm told you don't serve that."

"Breakfast is the most important meal of the day, Sam."

"Okay, Mom," she playfully teased.

They both stared at the center of the table. It seemed like neither of them knew what to say next. He placed his hands on the table and tapped along to a random Cyndi Lauper song on the stereo. "Blake," she whispered, drawing his attention to her eyes, "I wanted to apologize for the other day."

"Oh, um, that's really unnecessary," he said.

"No—it is," she insisted. "I have this really brilliant thing I do where I put my foot in my mouth." He watched her run her palm along her face. He noticed a tinge of pink staining her cheeks. It was the first time he had realized how pretty she was when she blushed. "It's actually a talent of mine, really."

With a sigh, he admitted, "I believe I may have been overly sensitive." As she tried to interject, he shook his head. "I have a tendency to shut down when discussing my dad," he said. "It's a defense mechanism, I'm sure, but I didn't mean to take that out on you."

"You're a good guy, Blake Forrester," she said, her voice filled with admiration. He chuckled nervously, running a hand through his messy hair, feeling the strands slip through his fingers. Looking up, her vibrant green eyes captivated him, although he didn't understand why her words affected him so much. He enjoyed being complimented by her.

"You're just saying that because you're around baseball playing whores all day," he said with a grin, adding a light chuckle.

She adjusted in her seat, leaning forward across the booth. Her perfume, a delicate blend of flowers and vanilla, wafted toward him. "Baseball players were never my type, anyway," she said, her voice tinged with a hint of mystery. Suddenly intrigued, he needed to know what Sam's type was. It was a question he had never asked before, an unexplored territory.

"So, you're telling me that tall, handsome, and rich is not Samantha Lancaster's type?" He shook his head with a snort. "Isn't that every woman's dream come true?"

Without taking her eyes off him, her cheeks blushed once more. She reached for a piece of toast and pushed it into her mouth. "I'm not every woman, Blake." He blinked, more than once, captivated by the way her eyes sparkled as she chewed her food. "But, if you must know, I prefer someone more down to earth."

"Is Casey a city boy, then?" He chuckled uncomfortably, the sound escaping his lips as a nervous release. He mentally scolded himself for even bringing up this guy's name.

She shook her head; the movement was accompanied by a soft rustling of her hair. Strands of dark tendrils fell across her forehead, and he had this inexplicable urge to brush them away, to feel the softness under his fingertips. He shook his head, trying to dismiss the peculiar sensation, shifting slightly against the plush cushion of the booth. "Actually, he's from a small town in Ohio." She shrugged nonchalantly. "But his ego is the size of Texas."

"Come on," he said, his eyes lighting up, "you had that crush on Jimmy when you were in high school. His ego was bigger than the entire school."

"I never liked Jimmy!" She crossed her arms, the movement creating a sense of defensiveness. The blush returned to her cheeks, a darker shade of pink.

"Sam, I think I would remember that. You told me your sophomore year," he said, the memories resurfacing within him. He recalled her sitting on the bleachers, her presence shy and reserved. He had teased her about which boy she was rooting for on the football team after they won that night. "We had just beaten Fairview, I think, and you told me you were rooting for Jimmy," he said with a gruff chuckle.

"You're an idiot," she said, a small giggle leaving her lips. "I never liked Jimmy my sophomore year."

"Then why did you tell me that?" he asked.

She shifted her gaze toward her lap, searching for the right words. "Oh, God." She swore nervously, fidgeting with the straw in her glass. "I had a crush on you, you idiot."

Blinking, he struggled to process her confession. Little Samantha Lancaster had a crush on him in high school? How had he never realized that?

"Me?" His question hung in the air for a moment before he laughed. "You're joking, right?"

"Do you think I would embarrass myself for laughs?" she said with a shrug, taking a sip of her soda.

"Honestly, I'm just surprised, that's all."

"Yeah, well, don't let it go to your head." She tossed a piece of her toast across the table, and he ducked before it could hit him. "It wasn't my fault. Blame it on my raging teenage hormones."

A grin spread across his face as he teased the table with his fingertips. "Is that your way of saying you were horny for me, Lancaster?"

"Oh, shut up!" she said excitedly, sitting up to playfully push his hands away from the table. "I spent enough time around you and my brother growing up to realize what a moron you were. Snapped me right out of it."

Before she could push him away, his hand closed over hers, and a jolt of electricity sparked between them. He caressed her palm, lingering on their point of contact. Swearing that his heart had suddenly started marching to a beat much faster than the current song blasting over his head, he released her hand, and she dragged it back into her lap. "I uh—I should get back to work."

She nodded, no longer making eye contact with him. "Yeah, I need to head to the hospital and check on Jax."

He rose, hesitating. "Dylan and I are meeting up at Boondock's at 8:00 PM for a beer. You should come."

He watched, mesmerized, as she nervously chewed on her bottom lip, a soft "Oh," escaping her mouth. Her pink lips, soft and supple, seemed to glisten slightly. "I don't want to crash your boy's night."

He nervously shoved his hands in his pockets and shifted his weight. "It's just a beer," he said with a scoff. "Or maybe you can't keep up anymore?" he teased.

"In your dreams!" she said sarcastically. Turning to leave, he heard her say, "See you at eight."

As Sam left the diner, he noticed the sway of her hips for the first time. His head tilt, as she rounded the corner, wasn't intentional—he wasn't trying to look her over—but he was still a man, and those jeans looked amazing on her.

To his annoyance, his sister's voice came from behind him. "Stop staring, loser." He quickly dashed away from her, back to his solitude in the kitchen.

For the rest of his shift, he focused on one singular thing. One thought he shouldn't be thinking about. He knew it was wrong. Yet the thought gnawed at him, a persistent itch he needed to scratch, so he knew he needed to get it out of his system. No matter how hard he tried, he couldn't stop thinking about the fact that he had made Sam Lancaster horny.

Chapter Seven

Samantha

S am flipped the pages of her magazine while she waited for her brother to come back from getting his X-rays, accidentally tearing the corner of the page. She cursed under her breath as she shoved the book back on the table. She had been fidgeting ever since she got to the hospital.

What was she thinking, telling Blake that she had a crush on him back in high school?

Raging teenage hormones! Way to go, Sam.

Why not just tell him you used to think about him in the shower while touching yourself? She groaned audibly.

"I missed you too, sis." Jackson's voice filled the air as his hospital bed wheeled into the room. He looked tired, but more alert than he had in days.

"Fancy meeting you here," she said, standing up as the nurse plugged in the various wires and tubes before exiting the room and leaving them alone. "So, how are you feeling today?" she asked.

"Like I hit a tree and almost died," he said with a lopsided grin and terrible humor. At least his attempt at jokes had her smiling.

"Too soon, Jax." She glared at him playfully but pulled up her chair and plopped down next to him. "Whiskey says hi, by the way."

"Can't you sneak him in here?" he asked, his lips turning down into a pout that looked ridiculous for a man his age. She swore that dog was the only thing that could bring her brother to his knees. Not even a woman could turn his eyes the way Whiskey did.

"No, I cannot," she said firmly. "But I have been taking him on a walk in the mornings."

His smile dropped. "Don't take him on walks. Are you insane?" He frowned, looking at the ceiling. "Now he's going to expect me to be active when I get out of here. Do you know how much I hate walking, Sam?"

"You can start with short walks when we get out of here. It's going to be part of your therapy." Opening her magazine and holding it in front of her face, she effectively ended the discussion. However, a question suddenly occurred to her, causing her to drop the corner of the page. "Hey, by the way, what's in Erie?"

She observed his face falling and a darkness in his eyes, prompting her curiosity further. "Erie, why?"

She shrugged. "Dad went there unexpectedly the other day and didn't explain why." Paying close attention to his reaction, she recognized his attempt to remain neutral. However, she knew her brothers had a tell when they weren't being honest with her. Dylan scratched his nose whenever he lied, and Jax tugged his ear. And right now, that earlobe was getting a big ole tug.

Trying to cover up, he replied, "No idea. Maybe he just needed parts for the shop."

Lying liar from Liartown.

Her eyes narrowed. "Hmm, parts, yeah, I suppose that could be true," she mused, glancing back at her magazine. "Except," she exhaled loudly, and Jax was really pulling on that ear now, "Dad's been acting off." Reflecting on her initial thoughts, she admitted, "When I first got here, I thought it was Dylan, being Dylan, but now I'm not so sure about that."

"Sam, can you just let it go?" Jax groaned, clearly annoyed.

Undeterred, she stood and leaned over his bed, determined to get answers. "Ah-ha, so there is something going on that you and Dad don't want me and Dyl to know about."

"Seriously, let it go, kid," he said, using a term that grated on her nerves. She despised being referred to as a child, as if she was not twenty-six years old. She was not willing to be dismissed so easily.

"Jax, I think I have a right to know if something is—" Her words trailed off as he turned his head on the pillow, signaling his disinterest in continuing the conversation.

"I'm tired, Sam. Can we not do this right now?"

She recognized the signs that the conversation was over, realizing it was best not to push her brother any further. However, she was far from finished seeking the truth. "Fine, I'll let you get your rest," she reluctantly agreed, "but that doesn't mean I'm done asking about it."

Sam walked into Boondocks at precisely 8:45. The dimly lit room filled with its dark wooden floors and rustic decor reminded her that nothing much changed in a small town. Overhead, the speakers were still rocking the same tunes from when she last recalled being here. The familiar sound of Bon Jovi's "Livin' on a Prayer" was playing from the jukebox in the corner. Loud music mingled with the laughter and animated chatter of the rowdy group of patrons playing darts at the back of the bar.

The bar still smelled the same. The overpowering scent of stale beer and cigarette smoke instantly brought her back to countless nights spent wasting time with her brothers and Blake here on endless Saturday nights. Behind the worn wooden bar stood Rusty, his face wearing a perpetually sour expression that concealed his naturally warm and friendly demeanor.

"As I live and breathe, is that little Samantha Lancaster walking into my bar?" Rusty said loudly as he placed his calloused hands on the worn wooden bar top.

With a confident stride, she crossed the room and hopped up on the stool. "Not so little that you ain't gonna serve me a whiskey and Coke, Russ," she said with a smile.

A smile cracked across his face, delighted to see her. "I wondered when you were gonna warm my stools and show these boys here how it was done," he said, glancing down the bar where Blake and Dylan sat, still unaware of her presence.

"You know, those two could never keep up with me." She winked at him as the glass clanked onto the counter. "Might as well make it a double."

Without hesitation, he tipped the bottle over and poured the amber liquor into the glass, sparingly adding soda before sliding it toward her. "Go easy on 'em," he said. "They've been having a tough time without your brother to show 'em how it's done."

"Never." She laughed, picking up her glass and confidently walking to the other end of the bar.

She walked up behind her brother and leaned against him, her arm resting on his shoulder. "Hey, losers."

His face suggested he did not know she would be coming tonight, and he responded with surprise, "Sam, what are you doing here?"

Blake, attempting to explain himself, stuttered, "Oh yeah, uh—I saw Sam at the diner today and thought it would be cool to invite her."

Dylan's brow rose suspiciously as he stared at them, before breaking the silence with a nonchalant, "Cool."

Blake swallowed anxiously and downed his beer in one gulp before turning toward her. "How's Jax?"

"Grumpy as always," she turned toward her brother, "and I think I finally agree with you. You're right."

A look of mock surprise crossed his face. "Wait, wait, you think *I'm* right about something?"

"Don't get cocky, asshole," she responded sarcastically. "But I think something is going on between him and Dad."

"I told you! Let's discuss after I go piss!" he said, clapping his hand against Blake's back with a resounding thud. He slammed his beer back and set the empty bottle on the counter. With a wave of his hand, he called out to Russ, "Another round." Sam quickly emptied her glass and set it next to her brother's bottle on the bar.

"Me too, Russ. Seems I need to show these boys how it's done." Dylan winked at her mischievously and excused himself to the restroom.

Blake, sitting at the end of the bar, stared at her intently, his eyes locked on hers as he nursed his beer. "You dance as good as you drink?" Blake asked, his words laced with a hint of curiosity she had never seen before.

She snorted, her hand coming up to cover her mouth. "I drink so I don't have to dance." Russ sat her drink down on the bar and she picked it up, taking a sip.

Blake stood up. He took a long drink of his beer before setting it down on the bar with a thud. He walked over toward her, his steps slightly unsteady. "Come on." He gestured with a nod toward the dance floor.

"Blake, no," she protested, her voice filled with a mix of hesitation and amusement. She watched as he grabbed her glass, the touch of his hand sending a tingling sensation across her skin, and placed it next to his beer.

He turned around and started walking backward toward the dance floor, his movements slightly clumsy. The adorable smile on his face had her heart skipping more beats than was humanly possible. "You're gonna make me dance by myself?" She did not know how much he'd been drinking, but she knew she wasn't drunk enough to miss him flirting. "Come on, Sam," he said, a playful pout twisting his lips as his eyes held a captivating glint. *Damn, he was adorable.*

He reached out and grabbed her hand again, the warmth of his touch enveloping her. She could hear the faint music of Aerosmith's "I Don't Want to Miss a Thing" playing from the jukebox. "Fine, but it's your fault if I break your toes," she warned playfully, trying to sound more apprehensive than excited.

His hand settled on her hip, sending a shiver down her spine as his fingers traced the skin beneath her shirt. She allowed him to pull her closer to his chest, swaying with him to the music. "I don't think you're big enough to break my toes, Sam." His voice was deep, and the warmth of his breath sent shivers down her spine, causing a cascade of goosebumps to rise on her skin.

Her heart raced within her chest as she gently glided her right hand up his torso, her palm pressing firmly against the firm expanse of the soft fabric of his T-shirt. The throb of his own heartbeat resonated against her hand. She struggled to maintain composure, trying not to succumb to the temptation of tangling her fingers in his silky hair with her left hand resting against his neck. As she shifted her hand against his skin, he stumbled slightly. Their eyes locked—his dark, intense gaze lingering on the contours of her face. She was almost sure she didn't imagine the way he leaned toward her.

"The hell are you two dancing for?" Startled by Dylan's voice, they sprung apart from each other. Sam steadied Blake by catching his arm as he stumbled backward. Blake recovered, standing next to her with his hands in his pockets. He stared past Dylan as Donna Draper stood glaring at them from a few steps behind her brother.

"It was a good song." Blake shrugged, as he strolled back to the bar to retrieve his beer. Sam followed closely behind, pushing past her brother and Donna toward the bar to collect her drink. Hopping up onto a stool, she wrapped her hand around her now lukewarm glass and swirled it before taking her own drink. She watched as Blake drank his beer, staring back at the bar.

Dylan joined them, carefully sliding into the vacant seat between her and Blake. "So, about Jax and Dad." The dance was seemingly already forgotten. Looking up, she noticed Blake staring at her with a distant expression she couldn't quite place.

The three of them engaged in conversation and small talk until they parted ways that night, as if nothing out of the ordinary had taken place. Yet despite two hours at the bar and the lingering effects of the alcohol, Blake's touch lingered on her skin. His haunting stare was the last thing she saw before she pinched her eyes closed and drifted off to sleep.

Sam woke the next morning with a smile on her face as she remembered her dance at the bar with Blake. Despite his slight inebriation, there was something thrilling about the way he looked at her. However, she scolded herself for getting her hopes up about Blake Forrester. She should know better than to fall for him after all the years of literally pining over him. He had never returned her feelings. This fantasy of hers would only lead to heartbreak.

It reminded her of a saying by a French philosopher: "The heart has its reasons, of which reason knows nothing." Who was she to defy her heart or reason?

Casey

Morning gorgeous

Casey

Thought you should know my bed misses you, and that makes my dick sad

The text from Casey was predictable. However, she left him on read and headed downstairs for breakfast. To her surprise, Dylan was still milling around the kitchen this morning. "Aren't you supposed to be at the shop?" she asked.

"Woke up late," he said, shaking his head at her cheerful demeanor. "I guess you really can still handle your liquor better than me." He popped two aspirin in his mouth and chased them with a glass of water.

"Whiskey's better for you than beer," she said with a relative sense of seriousness.

He snorted sarcastically. "I don't think that's scientifically true, Sam." She reached around him for the box of cereal and poured herself a bowl. "What was going on with you and Blake last night?"

As she reached into the fridge for the milk, her hand paused. "Going on?" She swallowed before shutting the fridge. "Nothing, Dyl. We were just talking. Just having fun."

"Yeah, well, it was weird," he said.

She rolled her eyes. "Okay, well, we're adults so—not sure what is so weird about two people dancing."

He waved his hands around dramatically. "Because it's you." Pausing for emphasis, he added, "And he's Blake." Standing in front of her, he stared intently, as if waiting for a response that would satisfy him. Breaking the silence, he quietly added, "He's my best friend, Sam."

"Okay," she said, her tone casual, "I was unaware that dancing was illegal."

Dylan's agitation suddenly became apparent. "Do you understand the complications here? If his dick even touched you, I'd have to kill him."

With a loud groan, she responded, "Oh my God, we danced, that's all." She didn't have time for her brother's anxiety attack, especially over something that was highly unlikely to happen. "I have to go," she said, her bag and cereal in hand as she headed toward the door. Before leaving, she turned back to deliver one last jab. "I'll be sure to text you photos if we start having sex."

As she shut the front door, the sound of crashing dishes echoed from inside the house.

Chapter Eight

Blake

B lake was sitting at the office desk, clicking his fingers against the keyboard of the computer. The numbers weren't matching in the register for the previous month. Frustrated, he took off his reading glasses and rubbed the bridge of his nose with his thumb and forefinger. Reluctantly, he considered reaching out to his mom for help with the finances, hoping she might know why the diner was missing $5,000. He hated bothering her with this stuff. It was his job to keep the diner budgeted monthly. With a sigh, he went back to the top of the register and started over.

Just then, Kelley slipped her head into the doorway, interrupting his concentration. "Hey, did you know we are out of napkins?" she asked.

Irritated, he pinched his eyes shut and replied, "Did you check the back room on the top shelf?"

Kelley shrugged and responded, "Duh, and the bottom shelf under the counter. Empty."

Frustrated by the situation, Blake tore open the bottom drawer and scanned the supply book. He traced each item they had ordered the previous month with his finger, and his shoulders sagged when he realized he had left napkins off the last order. "Dammit, I'm sorry Kels. It must have gotten missed. I'll get a rush order out today. Can you run to the market on your break and grab some until I can get it delivered?" he asked, feeling a tinge of guilt.

"Fuck yeah, I can," Kelley said.

Blake looked up at her with a scolding glance. "Seriously, Kels, how many times do I have to tell you to watch your language at work?"

"Sorry, boss." She sheepishly saluted and headed back to the counter to greet a customer.

Feeling overwhelmed, Blake closed his eyes and rubbed his temples with his hands. He wasn't sure how he missed the order, but it felt like he was screwing a lot of stuff up lately. Ever since he had gotten that notice from the Culinary Institute that he needed to decide on his enrollment or give up his scholarship, he seemed to be lost in his head.

The sound of bags crunching outside his office door distracted him. Looking up, he noticed his mother talking to his sister at the counter, carrying a bag of items in her hand. She then lifted the bag and brought it into the office. "Hey, Blake," she greeted him.

He groaned as she kissed his forehead and placed a can of iced tea on the desk next to him. "Hey, Mom."

His knee bounced anxiously under the desk as he leaned back in the chair, resting his head against the wood. "Why does my son look like the world is closing in on him?" she said.

He sighed and explained, "Any idea why we might be missing five thousand dollars?"

She laughed. "I don't think so." Pausing for a moment, she sat on the edge of the desk. "Wait, I had to pay to have someone come and check on the stove."

Confused, Blake glanced up at her. "When was that?" He couldn't recall any issue with the stove last month.

Sheepishly, she admitted, "I didn't want to worry you about it."

Frustrated, he groaned, "Mom, I need to know that in order to budget the cost." Their lack of communication had been an issue lately, and he didn't mean to get upset about it. However, he couldn't help but feel that it was really affecting his ability to do his job.

"I'm sorry, Blake," she said, realizing her mistake. "I just forgot about it, and you already have so much to worry about."

"Mom, I'm not a kid anymore," he shouted, observing his mother's face as it turned into a frown. He inwardly scolded himself for his outburst, taking a moment to collect himself. "I didn't mean to yell," he said, closing his eyes and taking a deep breath.

His mother's face softened. "It's fine, Blake. You're right, I should have told you."

Dismissing his mother's comment, he shook his head. "It wouldn't have mattered. I probably would have forgotten anyway, just like I did with the damn napkins." Perplexed, his mother looked at him, and he simply shrugged, trying to explain his scattered state of mind. "I'm just all over the place right now, but I promise I'll do better, Mom."

"Honey, you already do enough. You take care of this whole diner, you cook, you clean, manage the store, take care of your sister, make sure *I* take care of myself. Do me a favor and don't be so hard on yourself." She placed a hand on his shoulder, and he melted into her touch. "Why don't you get out of here for the day?" she suggested.

"Mom, my shift isn't over for two more hours," Blake said, protesting.

She laughed in that motherly way that always relaxed him. "As owner of Linda's Diner, I think I have ultimate authority on who goes home early." With a genuine smile, she gently pushed him toward the office door. "Besides, I saw Sam out there when I came in. Maybe someone's in need of a distraction?"

His ears perked up at the sound of Sam's name, even though he still wasn't sure what exactly had happened between them at the bar the other night. He couldn't stop thinking about it, about her. It was a dumb idea to flirt so shamelessly with her in front of Dylan. Alcohol tended to cloud his mind, making him braver than he should be. Or maybe it was dumber?

Because flirting with Sam Lancaster was about the stupidest idea he had ever had. She was Dylan's sister. It was breaking a bro-code rule. Relatives were off limits, and you were risking your dick to break that code.

His mother eyed him suspiciously as he sighed, realizing his resistance was pointless. He kissed her cheek as he reluctantly responded, "I'll see you tonight."

As he made his way toward Sam's booth, his mother called after him, "Have fun, Blake."

"Of all the diners in all the towns in all the world, she walks into mine," he said, muttering somberly. At that moment, Sam looked up from her book and their eyes met.

Her eyes danced playfully along his face, a smile forming on her lips. "Fancy meeting you here."

"I work here," he said smoothly, brushing a hand through his hair. "What's your excuse? Are you stalking me?" He let the line sit playfully, watching her cheeks color. He reminded himself that this was the stupidest idea he had ever had.

"Maybe." Her voice left a tingling in his ears. She teased her lip with her teeth, not backing down from his constant gaze.

He inhaled and asked the question he wasn't sure if he would regret or not. "You want to get out of here?"

Her eyes narrowed as she looked around the diner, almost as if she was expecting someone to be watching them and judging them for speaking to each other. "Sure, where to?"

"Since it was actually pretty warm out today, I was going to ride up to the clearing, unless you don't think you have the stamina," he said, his tongue darting out to wet his lips.

She shut her book and replied, "I don't have a bike."

"You can borrow Kelley's bike. She just lets it sit out back and go to waste," he said with a laugh. "She's apparently allergic to all forms of exercise."

"A girl after my own heart." She giggled. Her laugh was infectious, and he made a mental note to find other ways to elicit the sound from her going forward. She followed him outside toward the back of the diner, where he kept the bikes locked up. Something about this felt natural to him. He wondered if his reaction was because of knowing Sam for so many years, or something different entirely.

Sweat poured from his brow as he raced his bike down the path toward the clearing. Casting a quick glance over his shoulder, he noticed Sam was still keeping pace, her skin glistening with sweat. They were almost at their destination, a clearing that held a special significance for both of them. It was a place where they had found solace while growing up, and very few others ventured out this far. In fact, he hadn't seen anyone else in this spot for years until he ran into Sam after her return to town.

As he pulled into the turnoff, he skillfully swerved the bike to a stop, his foot hitting the dirt. Sam stopped nearby, kicking the bike stand and sliding off the seat. Bent over with her hands on her hips, she panted heavily. "Damn, Forrester, you didn't tell me we were racing."

"You're the one who told me not to go easy on you," he said with a grin.

She looked up at him, her brow raised, her mouth sitting agape as she tried to catch her breath. "That was before I realized you were such an enthusiastic rider."

He smirked, attaching his helmet to his bike. "I guess when you ride as often as I do, you just get used to it."

Sam stood up, unsnapping her helmet, her sweaty curls now sticking wildly to her face. She brushed her hand over her forehead, trying to sweep her hair off her skin as she caught her breath, and laughed. "Well, I am not used to that. In any shape or form."

"Guess you need to exercise more, Lancaster," he said with a grin. She shook her head at him, biting her lip, and he couldn't help but flash a flirty smirk. "Just trying to look out for you, you know."

She blew out a quick and fast breath, ignoring his flirtatious comment. "That was not exercise. I don't even know what *that* was."

"Just needed to blow off some steam," he said. "Had a bit of a shit day, if I'm being honest." The truth surprised him as it left his mouth. Normally, he wouldn't admit to anyone when something was bothering him, not even Dylan. They would just go to the bar and drink it off. But with Sam, something about her presence had him spilling his guts to her.

"Do you want to talk about it?" she asked, settling herself on the mossy rock by the creek. Her sea-green eyes bore into him, captivating him with their intensity.

He hesitated, glancing down at his shoes before speaking up. "No—yes, I don't know."

Her laughter blended with the soothing sound of the bubbling creek water. "Very non-committal. I love it."

He nervously bit the flesh on his nail bed, the weight of unspoken thoughts weighing heavily on his mind. These were the things he had kept locked away, unwilling to burden his mom or Kelley. These were things he wouldn't dare mention to Dylan because dudes don't talk about their feelings with each other.

"I'm pretty sure I'm a fuckup." He laughed at the way the words sounded coming out of his mouth. Sam simply blinked up at him, silently urging him to continue. "Lately, it feels like I can't do anything right. I even forgot to order the napkins for the diner last month, something I never do." He paused, his pacing mirroring the turmoil within him. "Kelley's been sneaking out of the house, and I didn't want to bother Mom with it. I thought I could handle it on my own, be a good brother, and let her figure things out. But she's not listening to me, and I don't know what's wrong with her. I'm afraid she might get hooked on drugs or end up as a prostitute, and I'll blame myself for it."

Sam snorted, quickly covering her mouth. "Sorry, please continue," she said, nodding curtly with a serious expression.

"Then the Culinary Institute messaged me about accepting or declining my scholarship. I know I won't move to New York, but having to decline it feels like tearing out my goddamn heart. It means giving up on a dream. And then I feel guilty for being upset about losing my dream because I'm staying here for Mom, and her only dream was my dad, who's dead. Like, really dead. So how can I even compare my pain?" He paused, placing his hands on his hips. "So yeah, I'm a fuckup."

She stood up and walked over to him, nodding her head silently until she spoke. "So that was a lot." He inhaled, his head falling back slightly as he closed his eyes. Suddenly, her hands were on his chest, and his heart sped up. "Blake, you aren't a fuckup," she said, as he opened his eyes. He was surprised by the sincere emotion looking back at him. "You're just overwhelmed by all the responsibility you have taken on."

"Yeah, didn't you learn anything from the movie's Sam? With great power comes—"

She closed her eyes and groaned. "Do not quote Spiderman to me, Blake." He chuckled. "You were just a kid when your dad died. I still remember watching how you took care of your mom and Kelley. You and Dylan barely hung out for months after that. You had just turned sixteen." She gently gripped his T-shirt between her fingers. "You should have been out partying and going on dates, but you were working the diner seven days a week and babysitting your sister at night. You were forced to grow up faster than most kids your age."

"I did what I had to," he said with a shrug.

"So cut yourself some slack." She patted his chest. "I think you are doing a great job." She grinned. "Who needs napkins anyway?"

"It is a widely accepted practice for customers to not eat like cavemen, Sam."

"Fine, but can we circle back to your prostitute, drug-dealing sister?" Her laughter once again filled the air, and he felt something warm inside of him. "Your little sister is not doing either one of those things."

"You don't know that," he said, trying to lighten the mood. "Trust me, she's a menace. The things that come out of that girl's mouth...I swear, if Sheriff Draper didn't already hate me, he's gonna find a reason to hate her."

"Do you want me to talk to Kelley?" she asked. "Maybe whatever is going on with her isn't something she wants to talk about with her big brother. Trust me, do you know how hard it was growing up with a dad and two annoying big brothers? I had to Google everything."

"I suppose it couldn't hurt," he said, considering the idea. He didn't want to involve his mom in it yet. He considered the possibility that her behavior stemmed from her recent graduation and that his worry was unfounded, and he was being too protective. But maybe Sam could get more out of her, female to female.

"Alright, so we've decided you're overwhelmed. Your sister isn't a drug-slinging whore," she said with a teasing grin.

"No, we decided you would look into it," he playfully corrected her.

"Fine, now can we talk about the fact you still keep denying yourself the opportunity to be happy?"

He stepped away from her, bending over to pick up a rock and skipping it into the creek. "I can't move to New York."

"No, you *won't* move to New York," she said, making a clear distinction. "Those are two different things."

"Anyone ever tell you how stubborn you are?" he asked, smiling at her.

She crossed her arms and pursed her lips, considering his question. "Just every damn day," she said.

He picked up a rock and aimed it at her feet, watching as it plunked down into the water, splashing up onto her legs. She squealed as the cold water hit her, jumping back from the splash. "You son of a—" She bent over, grabbed a stone, and slung it close to where he stood, splashing his knees with a stream of liquid. He sprinted away from the water, dodging her continued splashes, as he slung another stone toward her, water now dripping from her arms and legs. She stepped down into the muddy creek, her foot slipping against the mossy bed, and he watched as she slid toward the water.

Just before she tripped into the creek, he slid his hand against her arm, pulling her back as she crashed against his chest. "Woah there," he said, looking down at her dazed expression. A faint smile appeared on her lips but slowly faded.

Flirting with Sam was the stupidest idea Blake had ever had until this moment. Because now, as he looked down at her, the only thing he wanted to do was kiss her. She shivered slightly, his hand still firmly gripping her arm to steady her. He slipped his other hand around her waist, pulling her against him, and when she didn't resist, he loosened his grip on her arm. Her fingers gripped his T-shirt, balling like fists into the cotton fabric. He watched the rise and fall of her chest, his eyes trailing from her neck to her jaw, swallowing thickly the moment they landed on her plump lips.

He should just kiss her. Bro-code be damned. Their eyes met, and he could see her hesitation mirrored back at him. He should stop this. He should be the one to walk away. After all, she was Dylan's sister, for fuck's sake!

But then he flexed his fingers on her hip, brushing her skin, and a slight squeak sounded from her throat that undid him. To hell with Dylan.

He closed the distance between them, pressing his lips to hers. The moment she responded, opening her mouth to accept the slide of his tongue, a warmth spread from his head to his toes. One of her hands slid to the back of his neck, gripping his hair, similar to the way she did when they danced at the bar.

He could easily become lost in the movement of her lips, the way she fit so perfectly into his arms, or simply the sensation of her hair tangled around his fingertips along her back. Kissing Sam Lancaster was an experience unlike any other he had ever had. As her mouth slowed against his, he couldn't help but feel the absence of her lips as she pulled away. He opened his eyes, searching for hers. Her teeth worried a line against the flesh of her reddened bottom lip. Pressing his forehead against hers, their noses bumped awkwardly. "That was—uh."

"Yeah," she said lazily, a small smile forming against her lips. He gently brushed his thumb along her jaw as her eyes slid shut. "Probably shouldn't tell Dylan about this," she whispered.

He nodded, their foreheads still touching. "Bro-code and all," he agreed. "Probably shouldn't do it again, either."

"Every lawyer I know would advise against it." She inhaled deeply, looking up at him with her big green eyes.

He chuckled. "Do you know many lawyers?"

"Absolutely none." She took a deep breath.

He swallowed hard, licking his lips. "Me either." Their lips crashed together again in an urgent, needy kiss.

Chapter Nine

Samantha

S am walked through the aisles of the grocery store, practically floating on air. She was picking out random items to make dinner for Dylan and her dad this week. The reason for her euphoria? Blake Forrester had kissed her, and it surpassed anything she had ever imagined in her childhood dreams. It was the kind of kiss that could change a person's life, the kind of magical moment only found in romance novels. She never thought it could happen to her, but then Blake kissed her, and everything changed.

Now she felt like everyone who looked at her could see it, too.

When Mrs. Baker greeted her at the bakery that morning, as she set her German chocolate cake on the counter, the woman made a simple comment of, "Nice cake, miss." To which she only heard, "Nice Blake kiss."

After stuttering and turning three shades of red, trying to understand what the woman was saying, she hastily threw the money at Mrs. Baker before fleeing the store.

She barely slept all night, going over it all in her head. At one point, she even convinced herself that it had all been a figment of her imagination. But as she touched her lips and traced her fingers along her skin, she knew it had been real. She couldn't forget the way his mouth had devoured hers under the canopy of trees. Or the way his fingertips had touched her skin so delicately along the ridges of her spine, leaving a trail of goosebumps on her flesh.

Lost in her thoughts, Sam reached up to grab a box of spaghetti noodles and accidentally collided with another person's hand. Startled, she stepped back. "Oh, sorry—"

However, any good feeling she had at that moment was shattered by Donna's voice. "Hello, Samantha."

Sam closed her eyes and inhaled deeply before reluctantly turning to face the last person she wanted to see. "Oh, I wasn't aware carbs were something you could eat, Donna," Sam said sarcastically, trying to mask her discomfort.

"Some of us are blessed with a natural ability to maintain our figure," Donna replied with a smirk, delivering a snotty curtsy.

Sam shook her head in annoyance and pushed her cart forward, determined to ignore the girl. "It was great seeing you, like always, Donna," she said, trying to maintain a polite tone.

"I saw you with Blake the other night." The aggression in Donna's voice caused her steps to falter for a moment. When Sam didn't give her the attention she wanted, she added, "I hope you weren't thinking of starting something with my boyfriend."

Gripping the handle of her cart tightly, she turned toward Donna, ready to confront her. "Interesting," she said, her voice laced with skepticism. "Because he didn't even speak to you at the bar."

"Well, I like to give him his space when he's out with Dylan," she said with a tight grin. "So, this is me politely telling you that you need to back off."

Donna's response didn't surprise Sam; she had learned not to trust anything that came out of the bitch's mouth. Knowing her tumultuous history with the blonde, Sam knew Donna had a tendency to manipulate situations. "I'll take your advice into consideration," she responded with a tense smile, before turning and pushing her cart away from her.

Sam fussed over Jax's pillow while he grumbled and complained about the show on the television. Her mood soured after running into Donna at the supermarket. Her brother's attitude only made things worse. "Would you sit still, Jax?" she snapped.

He stared at her suspiciously, grumbling, "Is there a reason you're taking your bad mood out on my pillow?"

She tossed the remote back onto his lap and dropped into the chair next to his bed. "I'm not in a sour mood," she said with a pout.

Examining her closely, he made a grunting sound as he inquired with a tilt of his head, "So what's up then, kiddo?"

Scanning the room, she saw an opportunity forming. Maybe she could gather some information for herself and find out what was going on with Jax and their dad by playing a childhood game she enjoyed with her brother. Narrowing her eyes, she took her shot. "Truth for a truth?"

"Oh, the kitten has claws," he said, smirking. "Fine, I'm game. You first, sis."

She curled up in the chair, pulling her feet underneath her as she stared out the window. "I ran into Donna at the supermarket."

"Double D?" he said with a chuckle. "What did that bitch say to you now?"

She let out a satisfied laugh. It always comforted her to know that Jax had her back, no matter what. "She told me to stay away from Blake."

"I'm not surprised. Last I knew, they broke up, but they usually get back together before the fighting ends," he said as a low chuckle left his throat. "They're basically our town's version of Ben and J Lo."

She tried to smile, but her stomach felt sick. "How do you even know who J Lo is?"

"I don't live in a dungeon, you know," he said, shrugging, as she tried to fight off the negative voices in her head. "Why do you care about Blake and Donna, anyway?"

Staring down at her clothing, she absentmindedly picked at the stray string on her cardigan. "Doesn't matter," she said as Jax grunted, but his gaze remained fixed on her, scrutinizing every detail. "Your turn. Why were you up on Church Run Road the night of your accident?"

She noticed a slight flinch in his body and the tight clenching of his jaw as his ocean blue eyes diverted from hers. "I, uh—" He ran his hand through his hair, clearly flustered. "Shit, Sam, I was actually going to see Mom."

Confusion furrowed her brow. Jax visiting their mother's gravesite was unusual, but it also didn't align with the rest of Dylan's story. "Mom? But what does that have to do with Dad?"

"You asked why I was on Church Run, and I've told you. Truth for a truth. I was on my way to see her and got distracted. That's it." He reclined on his pillow, closing his eyes. "Are we done now?"

She leaned back in her chair, the invasion of new information churning in her mind, an impasse between siblings as neither one of them was willing to share more information. "Yeah."

Dylan chewed his food loudly from the other side of the booth while Sam scrolled randomly through her Instagram posts. Every few sentences, she would look up, nod, or add an extra "yeah" for good measure, just to keep the conversation moving. "There's no way I can keep up with the influx, though," he remarked.

"Sounds good," she said, her eyes drawn to a post of Donna posing on her front porch. Donna had her hair tied into a ponytail; her breasts pushed so far out of her top that there was almost no point in wearing one. She was awkwardly posing with the sun behind her, so the photo emphasized her breasts. Honestly, it would be hard to miss them, even in the dark.

Woke up like this, make it a blessed day! #NoFilter, the caption read.

She groaned, noticing that the photo had already received four thousand likes in just thirty minutes. Clicking into the picture, she immediately saw that Blake was one of the people who liked it, causing her to exhale and groan again. She clicked into Donna's profile, scanning through her grid and finding more of the same bullshit she had just been subjected to.

Donna's famous Double D's were on full display, but what struck her the most was the second most famous thing featured on her profile: Blake Forrester.

Blake and I at the Lake #Blessed

Look who surprised me with flowers and a date #BestBoyfriendEver

Trip down memory lane with Blakey #Love

Each photo caused another vile reaction, and her sour expression grew on her face.

"And then the doctor said I had six months to live, and I really think I'm going to just quit and move to Japan so I can train wild sea monkeys and live in a forest." Dylan's voice wafted over the loud vibration of the diner's rendition of Pat Benatar's "Love is a Battlefield."

"I think that's a good idea," she said with a deep sigh, biting her lip as she clicked out of Donna's profile before she did something stupid, like comment on one of her photos or, God forbid, accidentally like one of them.

"Okay, that's it," he said with a hint of frustration. She looked up and noticed Dylan staring at her, clearly annoyed. She realized she had been more distracted than she had initially thought.

Dropping her phone onto the table, she let out a sigh, "Sorry, I'm just distracted." As her eyes glanced toward the kitchen, she coincidentally caught sight of Blake emerging from the office. Their eyes met briefly, but she quickly averted her gaze and redirected her attention back to Dylan. "I, uh, talked to Jax yesterday about Church Run," she said.

"Oh, did he tell you why he was up there?" Dylan's interest was piqued as he sat up in the booth.

She nodded and replied, "He was on his way to see Mom."

A wave of emotions crossed Dylan's face, his confusion evident. "Mom? Why?" he asked, shaking his head.

She shrugged. "He wouldn't tell me anything other than where he was going. I tried to get him to tell me more, asked him what it had to do with him and Dad, but you know Jax, he shut down after that."

"Well, that's good. You got more out of him than I have," Dylan said, sinking back into the booth. "But if he was going to see Dad and ended up on Church Run to see Mom...Jax never goes up there, Sam." He paused, his gaze drifting out the window.

"I know," she whispered, her tone tinged with sadness. Out of the three of them, Jax was the one who took their father's lesson about emotion to heart the most. After their mom's passing, Jax had completely let her go. He never visited her gravesite or spoke about her. It was as if she had never existed.

Before she could react or excuse herself, Blake slid into the booth next to her. Startled, she flinched and slid further against the wall, trying to create space between them. "Sup, guys, how's Jax?" he asked, casually grabbing one of Dylan's fries and popping it into his mouth.

"I haven't been to the hospital in a couple of days. The shop is too busy," Dylan said, both men now looking at her.

Sam shrugged, engrossed in her phone. "He's doing fine," she said, feeling Blake's knee nudge her leg.

"Just fine. Are you doing alright?"

"Yep," she said, locking her phone and meeting her brother's gaze. "If you'll excuse me, I need to use the restroom and head over to the hospital." She dared a glance at Blake, who was looking at her with concern etched on his face. God, that face, with his strong jaw, piercing brown eyes, and those full and kissable lips. Why did he have to look so good? Swallowing, she glanced at him in irritation. "Do you mind?"

"Oh, yeah, sure." He stood up, and she brushed past him toward the restrooms, her heart racing nervously. The moment the door shut behind her, her shoulders collapsed against the cold tile wall.

Damn Blake and his stupid lips. Standing in front of the mirror, she stared at her reflection.

"Stop thinking about kissing him!"

Her reflection seemed to mock her, daring her to storm back out there and demand answers from Blake. How dare he kiss her and ruin everything she knew about kissing? What was she supposed to do now? It wasn't like she could go back to mediocre kissing.

Ugh! And why did it have to be Donna Draper, of all people? Donna didn't deserve Blake! Pouting, she felt the sudden urge to fall to the ground, kicking and screaming like a child whose favorite toy had been taken away. She looked down at the floor and scrunched her nose in mild disgust. Perhaps she could skip the tantrum and simply lodge a complaint with the diner about the state of their restrooms being not sanitary enough for her to have her melt down on their floors.

She took a deep breath through her nose, shutting her eyes tightly to compose herself. She would not let Blake Forrester get to her. She had spent years pining after him while he barely acknowledged her existence. She wouldn't fall apart now just because he had kissed her, even if it was a breathtaking, life-altering kiss.

Opening her eyes, she held her head high as she pulled open the bathroom door and stepped out, only to collide with something solid.

"I know you wanted to be discreet, but I'm not really one for bathrooms." Blake's voice resonated in her ear, causing her to groan and take a step back to create distance.

"I need to go," she said, trying to move past him. He leaned against the wall, blocking her path.

She sighed, feeling crowded. "Hey, what's wrong? Maybe I'm not the brightest guy, but I sense that you're avoiding me."

Their eyes locked, a fire burning within her that she struggled to control. "Listen, I just don't think this is a good idea."

"Is it because of Dylan?" His slight frown caused the corners of his eyes to crinkle, and she had to resist the urge to run her fingers along the soft lines on his cheeks. Shaking her head, she reminded herself that she was annoyed with him.

"No—yes," she answered quickly, maneuvering around him as he reached out and grabbed her wrist. "I don't have time for this," she said with a harsh sigh. "And honestly, I don't know how you do either." She blew out a breath, blowing a runaway curl away from her face as she stared at him. "Have a hashtag blessed day, Blake." Pulling her arm free, she hurried out of the diner, ignoring the disappointment that flickered across his face.

She couldn't find Dylan as she searched the parking lot of the diner. All she wanted was to drop him off at the shop and get back to the hospital to check on Jax. But why was nothing going right today? Her frustration was bubbling over into anger when she heard voices on the side of the diner. They were loud and angry.

Curious, she walked toward the chatter, but then she paused when her brother's voice suddenly shouted out clearly. *"Nothing is going on with my sister and Blake."* Startled, she tripped over her feet.

"Well, make sure it stays that way or else I'll have to have a little chat with your best friend about things he won't be happy about." Donna's threatening voice added intrigue to the discussion.

She thought she heard falling cans, and then there was a crash. *"I swear to God, Donna, this is bullshit. You knew I was drunk off my ass."*

"You're so pretty when you're angry, D." Donna's saccharine voice got quieter, and she didn't dare want to know what she and her brother were talking about anymore.

The atmosphere grew quiet, and Sam wasn't sure if she should peek around the corner or turn back when suddenly she heard her brother's voice loud and clear. *"Fuck off!"*

Startled, she pivoted and walked toward her car, racing to get safely behind the driver's seat before her brother turned the corner and started walking in her direction. She did not know what was going on between Dylan and Donna, or what any of that had to do with Blake. The situation was making her feel as crazy as her brother, with all the conspiracy theories her mind was drawing up.

The door slammed, and Dylan appeared beside her. "You alright?" she asked.

"Yeah, I'm good. Blake just asked me to take out the trash before I left." He scratched his nose and smiled, but her eyes narrowed on him.

These damn Lancaster boys, she thought. Smirking at her brother, she simply responded, "Well, isn't Blake lucky to have such an amazing best friend?"

Chapter Ten

Blake

B lake couldn't quite pinpoint what had changed between the time he had spent kissing Sam up in the clearing and seeing her at the diner the next day. It seemed like he had missed something along the way.

He knew Sam was concerned about what Dylan might think of their newfound connection, and he couldn't deny that the thought had crossed his mind as well. However, he had no intention of announcing it to his best friend just yet anyway, so he wasn't sure what the problem was.

When they had parted ways the previous night, their situation was still very much open-ended. They weren't dating, and he wasn't even sure if there was a proper term to describe what was happening between them.

But as he caught sight of her at the diner that afternoon, with her messy hair tied in a ponytail and clad in her brother's flannel shirt and an Alanis Morissette T-shirt, all he wanted to do was press his tongue to that spot behind her ear that made her moan so exquisitely.

However, when he approached her, he was met with a cold and almost angry demeanor. Blake might not have been the sharpest tool in the shed, but he could tell when a woman was mad at him, and Sam was definitely pissed.

The rest of his shift was spent racking his brain, trying to make sense of what had gone wrong. But nothing seemed to add up.

Feeling at a loss, there was only one logical course of action left for him to do. And it involved a lot of alcohol and his best friend.

He parked his bike next to the entrance pole at Boondocks and secured it with his lock. Dylan was supposed to meet him there after finishing up at the shop, so Blake thought he might as well get a head start on drowning his confusion away.

By the time Dylan emerged from the front door and made his way over to the bar, he had three beer bottles toppled on the table and an empty shot glass in front of him. "Geez, Russ, you let him drink all that alone?" Rusty only shrugged and placed a beer in front of Dylan before walking away to change the channel before the Steelers game came on.

"Took you long enough, man," Blake slurred, ending with a sloppy hiccup.

"The hell is wrong with you tonight?" His friend shook his head and scanned the bar. "Busy night in here for the game."

Blake, however, was not interested in the game; he just wanted to know why Sam was mad at him. "Did I shit on your sister or something?" The words rushed out of him without him thinking. "Piss her off," he corrected. "She seemed pissed today."

Dylan stared up at the television, and Blake noticed the tightness of his jaw. "The hell is up with your interest in Sam lately?"

"Nothin', just asking. I don't like it when people are mad at me, is all," Blake said, pinching his lips together and gesturing to Rusty for a new beer.

Dylan shook his head as he held the bottle of beer to his mouth. "You know Sam, she runs hot and cold." He swallowed his beer and then placed it on the counter. "But, uh, you should worry more about your own girlfriend, and, uh, less about my sister." His tone was firm, and Blake recognized it immediately as a threat.

At that moment, Rusty placed a beer on the counter between them, staring at the two friends with a bit of reservation. "You sure you should be drinking so much, Blake?"

"Are you gonna arrest me for DUI on my bike, Russ?" he asked. Rusty seemed to study him a little longer before walking away. Blake tipped his beer back, swallowing the cold liquid as he stared back up at the television. The National Anthem played, filling the room with a quiet atmosphere.

Glancing sideways at his friend, he broke the silence. "You do know Donna and I broke up, right?"

"You and Donna always break up. That never mattered before," he said, glancing upward in frustration.

Blake swallowed the truth of his words. It wasn't a lie; he and Donna had broken up and gotten back together more times than he cared to admit. But this time, it was different. Donna always manipulated her way back into his bed. However, he had reached his limit.

He finished his beer just as the Broncos kicked the ball down the field, signaling the start of the game. He stood, slapping his money down on the counter and leaning toward Dylan. "It matters this time."

As he walked toward the door, he heard Dylan's voice behind him. "You break that code, Blake; we're done." Closing his eyes and shaking his head, he continued out the door.

Blake could feel the sweat dripping down his forehead, tickling his brow, as he reached up with the back of his hand to clean his face. The sheer torture he was putting himself through this morning, working off the hangover from last night, had his legs burning. Leaning forward, he reached for his phone to turn up the volume on his music. As Guns N' Roses' "Welcome to the Jungle" sprung to life in his ears, his legs quickened their pace to match the punishing beat.

Bouncing against the small rocks and sticks scattered along the trail, his bike dodged and jumped at the obstacles in its path. Riding through the trail, lined with trees following Oil Creek, he could feel the stress of the last few days getting lighter with each passing moment.

Dylan's ultimatum had annoyed him. He understood the bro-code they had when they were horny sixteen-year-old teenagers, but things were different now. Not that he wasn't still horny as fuck, but Sam and Blake were both consenting adults. Who was Dylan to dictate what was or was not good for either of them?

He rounded the corner just as his bike hit a rock. Instantly, his tire spun out, and the ground give way beneath him. Cursing under his breath, he desperately tried to stop the bike from crashing sideways. Eventually, he skidded to a halt, breathing heavily. Leaning against the handrails of the bike, he removed his helmet and scrubbed his hand through his sweaty, unkempt hair.

In the distance, a dog's bark caught his attention. He scanned the trail ahead, kicking the pedal of his bike as he headed toward it. The sound of the barking guided him, but he already knew where he was going. He hoped the bark belonged to the dog he was expecting, and above all, he was eager to find *her* sitting on that mossy rock next to the creek. Finally, things seemed to be going his way.

As Whiskey came running toward him, he saw her sitting there with wide eyes. Climbing off his bike, he approached cautiously. "What are you doing here?" she asked. He realized he couldn't have everything he wanted today. She definitely didn't seem happy to see him.

"Hey, Sam," he greeted, patting Whiskey's head. With a sense of uncertainty, he walked toward the woman, who had defensively crossed her arms and positioned herself between him and the mossy rock.

"Did you follow me?" she asked angrily.

He couldn't help but laugh. "No, just riding off a hangover," he said.

"Can't you go bother someone else, like Donna or something?" she said, raising her chin and looking away.

He nodded in understanding, piecing things together. "Did Donna say something to you? Or Dylan?"

"No," she hesitated, "maybe—not that it matters. Why?"

"You might have moved to the city and forgotten what it's like to live in a small town, but around here, everyone likes to get into your business," he said, trying to explain himself as he watched her face. He could see her eyes sliding away from his before glancing back at him.

"Apparently, my ex-girlfriend—" He walked closer to her, placing his finger under her chin, gently lifting her face to meet his eyes. "Did you hear me, Sam? Because I need you to hear me when I tell you that my *ex-girlfriend* has a problem with boundaries." She swallowed, his fingers tracing along the softness of her neck. "I don't know what she or Dylan said to you, but I don't care about them, Sam."

"Blake, everyone says that you and Donna always end up—" Before she could finish her sentence, he pressed his lips against hers, a soft but firm kiss, and she hummed gently in response. When he pulled away, her eyes remained closed, her lips gently parted.

"Do you have anything else you want to protest or would you rather we return to—" She interrupted him by launching her arms around his neck, her lips bruising his as a smile grew on his face.

He took a step back and leaned against the nearest tree, firmly gripping Sam's hips as he pulled her flush against his body. Her fingers found their way into his hair again, a gesture that was slowly becoming a favorite of his. His tongue slid into her mouth, hot and wet, as he licked against her teeth, eliciting a moan from her. In that moment, he wasn't sure if it was her shivering or him. The guttural reaction sent him reeling, and he couldn't help but slide his hands under her T-shirt, feeling the warmth of her skin against his palm, which made his heart race.

As his mouth kissed her jaw, her hips ground against his, and he knew she must have been aware of the effect she was having on him. "God, Sam," he moaned against her ear, his tongue tracing along her lobe. His words or actions must have been right because her hands slid under his shirt, her fingers slowly trailing along his abs, leaving a burning trail on his skin.

Opening his eyes, he stared down at her, her green eyes dark with desire, her curly hair falling around her face as her messy bun came undone. Placing both palms on either side of her jaw, he kissed her fiercely, turning them around and pushing her back against the tree, his erection pressing into her hip. She panted into his mouth, her hands sliding along his back, hovering over the waistband of his sweatpants.

Suddenly, she pulled back, her head falling back against the bark of the tree, breathing heavily. "Wait, Blake," she panted.

"Waiting," he said with a cheeky grin, attempting to control his own breath.

"I'm not just going to have sex with you out here." She buried her head in his chest. "And we need to establish some rules."

"Rules?" She lifted her head, staring at him angrily, and he realized she was serious. "Right, rules, of course," he acknowledged.

"Dylan can't find out about this." She anxiously looked up at him. Did she really want to discuss his best friend right now? *Bye-bye erection!*

He took a deep breath, gazing up at the trees above him, and then nodded enthusiastically. "Logically, yes," he said. "No Dylan."

"No Dylan, or Jax, or my dad, or Donna," she said, and he was certain she would keep naming people until she covered the entire town.

"I'll be your dirty little secret, got it!" he said with a slight annoyance.

Her face fell, and she frowned. "Hey, I didn't mean it that way." Her fingers pressed against his jaw, and her lips brushed his chin. "Blake, I just really like you." He met her eyes and couldn't help but smile at the sheer sincerity in her words. "I kind of just want to keep you to myself right now."

"I really like you too," he said honestly, gently kissing her. "It is kind of hot, sneaking around." He put his hand against her back, pulling her closer. "Blake Forrester messing around with little Samantha Lancaster." He pressed his lips to her neck. "Did you ever think about it growing up?"

She licked her lips. "Only all the time," she confessed.

"Did you?" he said, grinning like a madman. "Care to share with the class, Miss Lancaster?"

She wrapped a leg around his calf, pressing herself against him. "Why?" she asked, looking up at him with anticipation. "Are you going to make my fantasies come true, Blake?"

He blinked and then stepped back, lifting her off the ground as she wrapped her legs around his waist. "That depends," he said, their kisses becoming wet and sloppy. "What will you be wearing?"

Her fingers carded through his hair as she looked down at him, a mischievous smile playing on her lips. "Do you still have your old football jersey lying around?"

Fuck, Samantha Lancaster was going to be the death of him.

Chapter Eleven

Samantha

It turned out that sneaking around with Blake was a lot more fun than she had ever imagined. During the day, while Blake was working, she would spend her time with Jax at the hospital. She made sure his physical therapy was on track, watched old episodes of Survivor as a form of distraction, and enjoyed making fun of the contestants who got voted off the island.

Although Jax was improving well, the doctors were struggling to make him understand that his recovery would not happen overnight. She also hadn't been able to get much information from Jax about her dad. Whenever she tried to bring it up, he would shut down and claim to be tired, using it as an excuse to take a nap.

Dylan, on the other hand, wasn't much help either. Ever since she overheard him with Donna, he had become cold and distant toward her. She wasn't sure what was going on with him, but she found herself avoiding him most days. While she could always sense when her brothers were lying to her, Dylan was the one brother who could tell when she wasn't being honest with him.

Consequently, she made it her mission to steer clear of him each day. She would wake up before him, rush off to the hospital, and find excuses to have lunch when he was busy.

Most of her free time was spent hanging around the diner, as it was the easiest way to catch a glimpse of Blake while he worked. And when she said, "catch a glimpse of Blake," she really meant to gawk and stare disrespectfully because, damn, he was still the sexiest man in Titusville.

Throughout the day, she found herself sitting at her booth, biting her nails, her eyes trained on his biceps or fixating on the way his tongue massaged his bottom lip while he concentrated on the task in front of him, she was anticipating the night he would use his tongue on other parts of her body besides her neck. She was finding it harder to concentrate as the week went on. Their nights together were becoming more heated, their make out sessions filled with a sense of urgency.

They were stealing away time in Jax's small cabin on the back side of her family's property. It was somewhere no one would expect to find them. However, their intimate moments were consistently interrupted. Just as things would heat up, Blake would abruptly stop, preventing them from progressing any further. This constant interruption was driving her to the brink of insanity.

She knew Blake desired her; his growing erection whenever they made out on Jax's couch made that much clear. Yet, his hands would only venture under her shirt, over her bra, but never any further. Meanwhile, his pants strained under the tension of his arousal. She understood Blake was a sweet guy, but he was far from a saint.

During a particularly heated make-out session two days ago, they had even discussed protection. Prior to this, Sam had always used protection with anyone she had been with. Considering Casey's history, she wasn't willing to take any chances. She knew there was always the high potential that she was not the only one getting an invitation to his mattress.

However, things felt different with Blake. She trusted him, especially since they had known each other for a long time. As they lay on the couch, warming themselves by the fire, they openly shared their sexual history. Sam felt comfortable knowing that her birth control was sufficient. If the time came with Blake, she wanted everything to feel natural. He had agreed with her, suggesting that he also saw the potential for something more between them.

So, there had to be something else holding him back, and she was determined to find out what it was.

"Hey Sam!" Kelley's cheery voice snapped her out of her lustful thoughts.

She smiled at the girl as she brought her a refill on her soda. "Hey, Kels."

Blake's sister grinned knowingly at her and took a seat on the other side of her booth. With a serious expression, she asked, "So, what did you do to Blake?"

Confused, she gave her a puzzled expression and responded, "Do to him?"

"I said the word "fuck" three times today, and surprisingly, he didn't scold me even once. In fact, he even brought me ice cream last night, which is something he never does." Kelley leaned forward in the booth, catching Sam's attention.

Sam narrowed her eyes at Kelley. "And you think that I had something to do with that, because?"

"Do you smell that?" she asked, leaning toward her. "That smell, God, it's so strong. Blake smells like it, too."

Sam, now interested, sniffed and asked, "Bacon?"

Kelley chuckled and explained, "No, it's that new love smell. The scent of lust and longing." She crossed her arms and smirked.

Sam's eyes widened in surprise. "I don't know what you mean, Kels."

Blake's sister nodded knowingly. "I thought you might say that. That was his response, too." She grabbed a fry and took a bite before continuing, "But I pay attention to people. I'm fantastic at it, and I'm onto you two."

She laughed nervously and changed the topic. "What are your plans now that you've graduated, Kelley?" Sam remembered Blake had wanted her to talk to his sister, so perhaps she could at least gather some information.

"Nice change of topic. I like you." She nodded in approval and added, "I'm not really sure yet. City college, most likely." Just then, Donna Draper and her friends entered the diner, causing Sam to sink slightly into her seat.

Kelley glanced at the group and shook her head before saying, "Double D. Chicks can be dicks."

"That they can," Sam agreed with a smile, acknowledging the truth in Kelley's statement.

"Anyway, city college is probably fine. I can't see going anywhere else. It doesn't seem fair." She looked back at her brother, who was now observing Sam's interaction with Kelley. "He's probably pissed I'm sitting down on the job," she said. Standing up, she grabbed her empty glass. "Whatever you're doing—or not do-ing—I approve." With a grin, she walked away, sneering at Donna and her friends as she passed their booth.

Blake's hands gripped her hips, his fingers digging into the den-im of her jeans as she ground against him. Her tongue licked a strip along his jaw, enjoying the soft moan he whispered against her ear. As she nipped his earlobe, his hands slid under her shirt. Her heart sped up as she leaned into his touch. Fingertips scorched a trail on her flesh, skimming just under her bra.

Almost there, big boy, just a little closer.

Her body had been aching for his touch for days, yearning for his fingers to slip where she wanted them. However, just as he was about to fulfill her desires, his hand withdrew from her shirt, sliding up her back.

Frozen, she couldn't help but let out an audible groan of frustration. She sat up, staring him down. "Are you allergic to my breasts?"

He opened and closed his mouth a few times before shaking his head. "No, of course not."

Confused, she pressed further. "Then what the hell, Blake?" She climbed off him and pushed his legs off the couch, settling into the cushions. "You act like you want me, but then you just...stop." She frowned. "Did I do something wrong?"

Adjusting himself and sitting up further on the couch, he ran his hand through his hair before responding. "You did nothing wrong, Sam, it's just...Fuck." Frustrated, he groaned. "This is going to sound so stupid."

Reassuringly, she slipped her hand into his, intertwining their fingers. "You can tell me anything. I'm not going to judge you."

Laying his head on the back of the couch and turning to face her, he smiled as he reached over and brushed her hair idly from her face. "I want you so bad, sometimes I feel like I'm going to burst—but..." He paused, causing her to laugh nervously.

"It's never good when there's a but."

He took a deep breath. "Sometimes when I'm touching you, I feel like I'm corrupting little Samantha Lancaster and Jax and Dylan are gonna burst through the door and beat my ass."

She snorted, her laughter bubbling up inside of her as she realized he was serious. "So, you won't touch my breasts because you're afraid you'll corrupt me?" she asked.

"When we were growing up, you were untouchable. It wasn't even an option," he said, a smile on his face as he touched her knuckles to his lips.

She sat up and crawled onto his lap and looked down at him. "So, you never looked, not even once?" She desperately wanted to know the answer.

"Sam," he said with a loud groan, a desperate frustration in his tone.

The corner of her lip turned upward playfully. "That wasn't a no, Forrester," she said with a giddy smirk.

"I didn't say I never looked," he admitted, a lazy grin on his face. "You walked around in those skimpy shorts all the time. I was seventeen years old; I was a walking hard on. What did you expect?" Her cheeks warmed at his words. She wiggled in his lap, and he placed his hands around her waist to still her.

"So, you might have looked at me a few times." She giggled.

"Dylan would have my dick if he knew that." She bit her lip and ran her fingers down his chest until she reached the top of his jeans.

With a naughty grin, she looked down at his lap and let her hands slide against the bulge in his pants. "This dick?" she asked, her voice filled with mischief. He swallowed hard and nodded, unable to find the right words. "What would Dylan say now if he knew you had seen my tits?"

She reached for the hem of her T-shirt and pulled it over her head, tossing it to the floor beside her, revealing her white lace bra. She could see his chest rise and fall quicker. "Fuck, Sam," he said breathlessly.

Her next move came naturally as she reached behind her, swiftly twisting the clasp of her bra and unsnapping it. The lacy material loosened against her skin, and she slid the straps down her shoulders until her bra fell to the ground, joining her T-shirt. Blake's eyes wandered away from hers, his gaze fixated on her body as his mouth hung open. In response, she subtly pursed her lips and tilted her head, silently challenging him.

Staring him down, she licked her lips as she provocatively declared, "Your move, Blake."

He slid his hands up and down her arms, sending goosebumps along her skin. "Those are some beautiful breasts, Sam," he said, his eyebrow lifting playfully as the corner of his mouth turned upward.

She smiled in response, taking his hands in her palms and placing them both flush against her breasts. Inhaling sharply, she asked, "How do they feel?"

His eyes darkened, the playful banter now gone as his hands squeezed her flesh under his palms. She moaned, her eyes falling closed as her fingers slid between the digits of his own. She relished in the way his warm hands felt on her body, teasing her nipple with his thumb and forefinger, watching her intently as his eyes stared into hers. "Is that what you want, Sam?" he asked, his voice hoarse and low.

She nodded, his smile growing. However, she wouldn't let him undo her just yet. "Yes," she said with a loud groan, gathering the last string of control she had remaining.

Suddenly, he sat up, his hand sliding up the side of her breast as his eyes remained on her face. His hand slipped to the back of her neck, pulling her down to his face and her lips pressed against his mouth. And in that moment, the string snapped.

Their tongues clashed in a fight for dominance while his hand clutched at her breast. As their breath mingled and they panted against each other, he kissed a hot trail along her neck and pressed soft kisses on her collarbone. Tilting her head back, she felt his arms wrap around her back as she let out a soft moan. His tongue circled her breast, sucking her nipple into his mouth while his teeth grazed her flesh.

Rocking her hips forward, she slid along the delightfully large obstruction between them, delighting in watching him fall apart beneath her. "Sam—"

His hand traveled lower down her body, reaching for the button on her jeans. With a flick of his thumb, he had it undone and slid his hand into the front of her pants. The palm of his hand pressed firmly against the apex of her thighs. "Do you want me to touch you here too, Sam?"

Did she know words right now?

Her head felt hazy as her arms wrapped around Blake's neck, fingers buried in his dark, thick hair while he nipped at her breasts. Glancing up at her with mischievous eyes, she bit her lip. She pushed him back against the couch before detaching herself from him and standing. With a smile, she watched him as she slowly slid her jeans down her hips, shimmying them past her knees until she stepped out of them, leaving her just in her white cotton panties.

Placing her hands on her hips, she frowned. "Is there a reason I'm the only one doing show and tell?"

In response, he sat up quickly, ripping his T-shirt over his head and throwing it somewhere on the other side of the room. He stood up and undid the button of his jeans. She stared at his chest, trying not to get impatient and jump his bones. With his jeans discarded, he was left standing in his boxers, his lips parted, his eyes locked on hers.

Breaking the silence, she stepped closer to him, her hands tracing the ridges of his abs, following the trail of hair that disappeared down his stomach. Her voice filled with desire, she confessed, "I've been dreaming about this moment since I was sixteen years old." As she slid her hands into his boxers, she closed her eyes, relishing the moment she felt the silky hardness of his cock. Overwhelmed with anticipation, she boldly declared, "I think I might physically die if you try to stop me now."

He groaned softly as she stroked him in her hand. "Sounds dramatic, but I'm not going to...to argue with your logic." His words stuttered as she slid her fingers over the tip of his cock, his eyes pinching shut, unable to contain his pleasure. He hissed in response.

Sensing his surrender, her other hand went to his neck, pulling him down to her mouth. She nipped at his bottom lip, teasing it between her teeth, while her desire grew. "Do you want me, Blake?"

His fingers instinctively dug into her hip, sliding down to grip her ass. Suddenly, she was being lifted and dropped onto the couch. He looked down at her with a huge grin, his excitement growing. "I think I can do better than what sixteen-year-old Sam Lancaster could imagine." With that, he slid his boxers off, leaving him in all his glory. And damn, he was right. There was no way she could have ever imagined *that* at sixteen. He was perfect.

He bent over, slipping his fingers into the sides of her panties. Slowly, almost torturously, he slid them down her legs. His fingers brushed against her ankle, and he kissed his way up to her knee. Settling between her legs, he gazed up at her and smirked. "I've changed my mind," he said. "I think I should have corrupted you sooner."

Playfully, she pushed his shoulder with her foot. He firmly gripped behind her knee and pulled her toward him on the couch. She giggled loudly, until she felt his mouth press against her center, his tongue sliding between her folds. "Oh, God!" she squealed, squirming beneath him.

His hand gripped her hip, holding her in place beneath him as his other hand softly traced her inner thigh. His tongue teased her, pressing against her sensitive nub. Overwhelmed with pleasure, she reached out and gripped his hair, pulling him closer. She could sense his smug smile, because of course he would not only be talented at this but also cocky as shit. With each lick, each stroke of his tongue, she felt herself unraveling.

His fingers slid into her, moving inside her with a slow, fluid motion. "Blake, please..." she begged, though not entirely sure what she was pleading for, but desperately needing it nonetheless. He responded promptly, sliding a second finger in and using his thumb to press on her most sensitive spot. Everything else faded away as she pulled on his hair, crying out his name as the pleasure overtook her, arching off the couch as she gripped the strands of his hair desperately between her fingers.

When she finally settled back against the couch, she opened her eyes to find Blake staring at her with an expression of awe. "That was—wow," he said, shaking his head. "I don't think I've ever seen anything like it."

"Shut up." Her hands covered her face as she felt the flush of warmth on her cheeks, and he gently tugged them away.

"Don't hide, you're beautiful." The mood changed. The air felt charged, as things suddenly turned serious. He slid up her body, pressing her breasts firm against his chest, and his lips touched hers gently. "I want you so badly, Sam."

It was the hottest thing she had ever heard. Blake Forrester telling her he wanted her. She may as well die and go to teenage heaven because this was every girl with an unrequited crush living out her dream.

"Are you still good without a condom?" he asked, interrupting the moment. She gazed up at the ceiling, realizing her track record of being responsible and always using protection, but they had discussed this. And she wanted him, all of him. Just him.

"I just want to feel you." Their eyes connected. The air charged as he leaned over and pressed his mouth against hers. He shifted his weight, maneuvering between her legs, and she felt the weight of his hardened cock against her thigh.

This was really happening! She was about to have sex with Blake Forrester. She had fantasized about this moment every day in high school, and now, as if she had hit the sex jackpot, it was becoming a reality.

Her chest rose and fell rapidly as she breathed through her nostrils, gazing at the top of his thick brown hair as he focused on positioning himself. Lost in the moment, she slid her fingers into his hair, gently pushing it away from his face.

She watched the intense stare of his eyes, the tense tick of his jaw. Her palm cupped his cheek, pulling his face upward until his eyes met hers, dark brown orbs locked onto the green of her own intense desire. "Stay here," she whispered, drawing his attention to her.

He lowered himself, his mouth meeting hers as she felt him, hard and throbbing, slide into her. For a moment, she closed her eyes tightly, but quickly opened them when he moaned her name, watching him as he fully entered her with an erotic groan. Suddenly overwhelmed by the intensity of his gaze, she reached up and pulled him down by the back of his neck, his teeth grazing against her jaw. "Oh God, you feel so good, Sam," he uttered, his eyes fixated on her.

With her legs wrapped around him, she pulled him deeper, and he rhythmically moved his hips against hers. "Blake," she sighed seductively, her voice growing closer to climax. Her fingers dug into his shoulder as he thrust harder into her. He gripped the thigh wrapped around his waist, lifting it higher, intensifying their connection. The angle hit a spot that had her screaming out his name.

"Fuck, I'm not gonna last much longer," he admitted, bending down to slide his tongue into her mouth. As he did so, his hand slipped between them, his fingers gliding through the wetness of her center. He breathed against the corner of her mouth and whispered, "Come for me, Sam." The sound of his voice, his hands on her body, and his cock buried inside her pushed her over the edge.

She tightened around him, her eyes pinched shut as a loud groan escaped her lips. White light exploded behind her closed eyelids, as if the entire world had stopped.

When she finally opened her eyes, she found his eyes shut tight, his mouth slightly ajar. He continued to thrust into her with reckless and sporadic movements until, finally, his head fell against her shoulder, and he panted heavily as his own orgasm hit him.

She lay there, her body completely wrecked from the best sex she had ever had in her life, staring up at the ceiling of Jax's cabin. Uncertain of what to do next, she couldn't help but imagine all the "what if" doom scenarios running through her head at once.

What if he hated having sex with her?

What if now that they had sex, this whole fantasy shattered

What if Dylan really did burst through the door and beat his ass?

What if this ruined everything?

What if she fell in love with Blake Forrester?

Chapter Twelve

Blake

B lake had never done drugs before. He had never even smoked pot in high school. Although he enjoyed drinking beer and occasionally indulged in a decent whiskey sour, he always considered himself a moderate drinker. He never did anything too extreme. Until now.

Blake Forrester was addicted to Sam Lancaster.

There was no other explanation. She consumed his thoughts, invaded his dreams. Hell, he was jerking off in the shower every morning before work simply because of the hard on that dreaming about her was causing. Something inside him had broken after having sex with Sam—that was the only conclusion he could come up with.

Throughout the workday, his mind was fixated on finishing work so he could have sex with Sam at Jax's cabin after his shift. Even on his ride home after being with her, he couldn't help but look forward to waking up the next day to repeat the cycle.

Maybe there was some sort of support group for losers like him, where he could get help for his addiction. He couldn't exactly confide in his best friend, as it would violate the bro-code that had been in place since they were eleven. Blake felt like he was damned for what he had done, but the addiction had such a powerful hold on him he didn't seem to care. In fact, he would proudly wear a T-shirt if Sam allowed him, labeling himself as the founder of the "I fucked Sam Lancaster Club."

Maybe that was not his best idea.

No matter what, he was guilty of breaking the code, and he would willingly accept the consequences. Being with Sam brought him more happiness than he had experienced in years. The past two weeks since they had gotten together had been unexpected and exhilarating. Whether it was sneaking off to their secret spot with Whiskey, hiding out in Jax's cabin, basking in the warmth of the fireplace while naked, or simply sitting in a booth at the diner, discreetly touching knees under the table when no one was looking, these were the moments he eagerly anticipated every day.

Having Sam all to himself was a joy, although a part of him felt envious that Jax would be returning home from the hospital soon, meaning Sam would spend more time assisting with his recovery. This would make it more challenging for them to find alone time. While Blake recognized that using his friend's home for their intimate encounters was inappropriate, and considering she was also that friend's sister, he could no longer ignore the growing selfishness he was feeling about Sam.

With Jax's imminent return home, Sam's time in Titusville would also be drawing to a close. Blake always knew their relationship had an expiration date, but Jax served as a stark reminder that their connection was purely temporary.

"I'll be your dirty little secret."

He had only half-meant it when he uttered those words, but now they resonated as a painful truth. Perhaps Sam only wanted him for sex, a distraction while she tended to Jax in town. After all, why would she want a relationship with a small-town nobody after she returned to the city and had access to all her hot, wealthy ball players?

He recognized he was spiraling when he burned his fifth piece of bacon. Realizing this, he loudly announced to nobody in particular, "I need a break," before pulling out his phone and sending a desperate text.

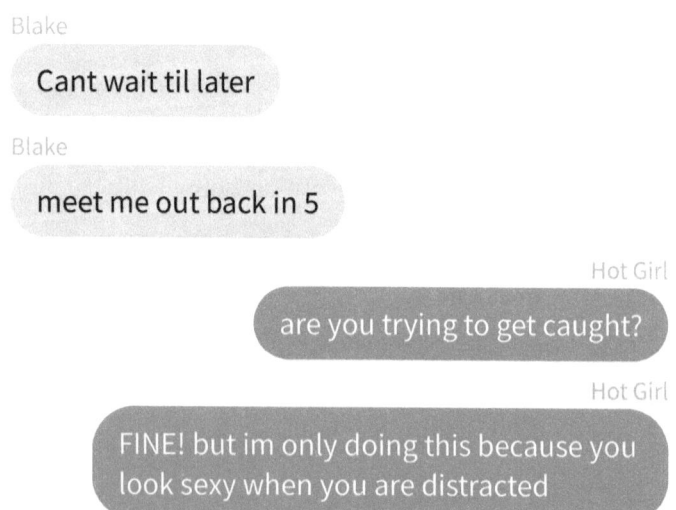

Blake

Cant wait til later

Blake

meet me out back in 5

Hot Girl

are you trying to get caught?

Hot Girl

FINE! but im only doing this because you look sexy when you are distracted

Blake swiftly shoved his phone into his pocket and made his way through the back door of the diner. As he stepped outside, he kicked the door shut, relishing the cool air that greeted him. His face was still flushed from the intense heat of the grill and the overheated kitchen. Disposing of the bag of trash, he tossed it over his head and into the dumpster, forcefully slamming the lid shut. Leaning against the back wall of the diner, he closed his eyes and took a deep, calming breath.

Feeling the need for distraction, he pulled out his phone and began scrolling through his social media feed. However, most of the posts comprised of desperate attempts by Donna to grab his attention, resorting to posting thirst traps on Instagram. Unfortunately, he realized that in the past, this tactic would have worked on him.

Since spending time with Sam, he realized Donna was merely a means to alleviate his boredom in this town, preventing him from hating himself. Yet, he had finally realized that being with Donna only fueled his self-loathing. She embodied everything he despised—self-centered, narrow-minded, rude—and she showed no genuine care for him or his family. He had been so gullible in the past to fall prey to her bullshit manipulations and whining that had him running back to her every time he had gained the courage to end things with her. He hated himself for ever falling into that trap.

Just as he was putting away his phone, Sam appeared around the corner. With a mischievous grin, he swiftly approached her and grabbed her hand, pulling her toward him until she was pinned against the wall. "If you keep burning the bacon in there, this town might rise up with pitchforks," she said playfully.

As his lips brushed against her jaw and trailed up to her ear, he mumbled, "Bacon increases the risk of heart disease, so really I'm doing them all a favor."

Their lips met, needy and fast. It was the kind of kiss that sent tingles down to your toes. He pressed firmly against her, pushing her into the wall, savoring the sensation of her fingers sliding under his jacket and pressing against his shirt. Moaning into her mouth, he felt her lips curl into a smile. "Steady there, tiger," she said with a sly smile.

"You drive me crazy," he whimpered, his tongue tracing the contours of her neck.

"Oh."

A sound broke the passionate atmosphere, leaving them wide-eyed and staring at each other before turning toward the new intrusion. Kelley stood at the back door, her brow lifted, a small smirk playing on her lips.

"Sorry, I was just going to ask if you needed an energy drink, but clearly you are energetic enough," she said, her eyes playfully glancing down his body.

"Go inside, Kelley," Blake snapped. His sister shrugged and turned around; the door slamming shut behind her.

Leaning his head on Sam's shoulder, he sighed, "Shit, sorry about that. I'll talk to her."

There was a moment of silence, broken only by the sound of their breathing. "She suspected something anyway," Sam finally whispered.

Lifting his head, he stared at her in disbelief. "What? Since when?"

"Last week, maybe even before that," she said with a shrug.

He shook his head, amazed. "She's a menace, I swear."

Blake placed his bookbag on the couch before tiptoeing through the living room. It was late, and he didn't want to wake up the house as he snuck back in after spending most of the night with Sam at Jax's cabin. As he crossed through the kitchen, the floorboards creaked beneath his feet, and suddenly the light from the refrigerator illuminated the room.

He practically jumped out of his shoes. "Shit, Mom, you scared me!"

His mother laughed, pulling out the remnants of leftovers and setting them on the counter. "I figured you might be hungry when you got home, so I saved some food from dinner."

Blake responded, "You didn't have to do that." His stomach said otherwise as he made a plate and set it in the microwave. "But thank you."

His mother stood silently, watching him from the other side of the counter. "You seem happier lately," she said, observing him.

"Mom." The warning tone cutting her off in his voice.

She shook her head. "What, can a mother not make observations?" The microwave beeped, and he busied himself preparing his food, sitting down at the table to enjoy his late-night dinner. His mother joined him, lightly touching his hand with hers. "I just meant to say that you seem less anxious, more settled," she said.

His fork paused on his plate. With Sam, he did feel less anxious. She relaxed him, and there was something about being around her that made him feel comfortable. He nodded, his silence the only answer.

His mother stood up and ran a hand through his hair, patting him on the back. "Tell Sam she can stop by when I'm at the diner, too. I'd love to catch up with her," she said with a knowing smile.

As Blake's mother went to bed, he felt his heart sink slightly. The knowledge that both his mother and his sister were aware of his relationship with Sam made it feel more real to him. Surprisingly, this part didn't bother him. In fact, it was quite the opposite—he felt relieved.

He envisioned bringing Sam to the house and taking her on an actual date, even holding her hand in public. It was then that he realized he wanted Sam to be his girlfriend, not just a friends-with-benefits situation.

However, he didn't know how to approach this with her, as she had been clear from the start about what she wanted. Additionally, there was the whole issue of Dylan. Perhaps his mom and Kelley's reactions had given him a false sense of security regarding how everyone would react to him and Sam being together. Would it be too much for him to expect Dylan to welcome him with open arms, a pat on the back, and a cold beer?

As he sat in the dark, Blake shook his head with a desperate laugh. He knew deep down that Dylan would definitely not react that way.

Still, he held onto hope.

Blake tightened the coat around Sam's chest as they ventured out into the chilly morning. "It's getting colder out in the mornings," he said, his voice filled with concern. "Soon we are going to have to take these walks later in the day."

Whiskey bounced at their feet, tugging at the leash, eager to explore the trail ahead. Sam looked up at Blake, blinking her lashes at him. "I know," she said, a hint of disappointment in her voice. "But with Jax coming home from the hospital this weekend, we won't be able to use his cabin."

A small pout formed on Sam's lips, prompting Blake to lean in and plant a gentle kiss on her mouth. "Don't sulk," he whispered affectionately. "You know I can't resist you when you do that."

Blake pulled away from Sam, intertwining their fingers as they followed Whiskey down the trail. Their hands swung between their bodies, creating a warm and comforting sensation. Sam hummed beside him, and Blake recognized the tune as a Taylor Swift song, often played loudly by his sister in the early morning hours. He was pretty sure it was something to do with High School.

"Feeling nostalgic?" Blake playfully nudged Sam with his shoulder.

Sam stared at him wide-eyed before bursting into laughter. "Are you a secret Swiftie?"

He laughed. "I have a little sister, Sam."

She shrugged. "I guess I'm feeling sentimental." He squeezed her hand tighter, feeling a surge of happiness. "Did you know I wrote our initials on a tree in the clearing back in high school?"

Now it was his turn to be shocked. "You did not!"

"I did." Sam giggled mischievously. "I told you my crush on you was huge."

He regretted the fact that he had never realized how much she had liked him when they were growing up. It made him wonder often about how he had missed all the signs. If only he had paid closer attention to the glances she gave him, or the comments she made, perhaps he could have seen her true feelings sooner.

As they reached the clearing, she broke away from him and headed toward a cluster of trees. "Here it is," she said. He followed her across the creek, stepping carefully around a large rock and positioning himself beside her on the other side of the tree. His eyes fell upon the bark, where he noticed the old letters scratched into the wood: SL + BF.

"Wow," he said, wrapping his arms around her waist and resting his chin on her shoulder. "You really did have it bad, Lancaster." Curiosity got the better of him. "When did you do this?" he asked.

"I was sixteen," she began, but then quickly covered her face. "No, I don't want to tell you." He shook his head, determined to hear the full story.

"Well, now you have to tell me," he insisted, gently pulling her hands away from her face.

She looked back at him, a slight frown on her face. "Fine, but you can't laugh at me," she warned.

He smiled sincerely. "I couldn't make fun of you if I tried," he reassured her, though he couldn't help but crinkle his nose playfully. "Alright, fine, maybe a little."

"Do you remember that night after graduation when you and Dylan came home drunk, desperately trying to hide from my dad?" she asked, scrunching up her nose. He furrowed his brow, trying to recall the memory. "And I caught you guys out back, attempting to sneak in," she continued, a mischievous smile on her face.

Suddenly, the memory flooded back to him—a younger Sam, just sixteen years old, standing in the backyard, threatening to turn them in as they tried to bribe her to keep quiet.

"Oh my God, I think you cost me fifty dollars that night," he said, his tone a mixture of amusement and disbelief.

"You kissed me that night," she said softly, causing his eyes to widen.

"I did what?" he asked, attempting to recall the events of that night. It was mostly a blur, but he was certain he would have remembered kissing his best friend's sister. "I did not."

"Granted, you were very drunk, and I did bribe you," she said with a soft chuckle, sounding quite pleased with herself. "And when you handed over the money, you pressed a kiss to my cheek, and I might have turned and kissed your lips."

"So, you took advantage of me in my inebriated state?" he asked, feigning shock.

She simply shrugged. "It was my first kiss."

Suddenly overwhelmed by her confession, he couldn't help but ask, "I was your first kiss?"

"Yes, you were drunk," she began, slightly unsure of herself but also sounding a bit proud of the whole ordeal. "But after that, the next day, I came out here and did this." She pointed at the tree, her words punctuated by a gesture. He bit his lip, torn between conflicting emotions in the present moment. He wasn't sure if he should feel offended or turned on.

"Do you know what I always wanted to do back then?" she asked, turning in his arms to face him. He looked at her with mild amusement, intrigued by her question. A smirk played on her lips as her fingers danced lightly on his chest. Suddenly, she flipped them around, forcefully pushing him against the tree, his back hitting the rough bark.

"Take advantage of a poor, drunken teenager?" he said playfully.

"Sort of," she answered, her voice dripping with a mischievous tone. Licking her lips seductively, her hands trailed down his chest, eventually reaching for the waistband of his sweats. A shock of coldness ran through him as her fingers slipped into his pants, her small hand gripping his cock firmly.

"God, Sam," he said, unable to contain his pleasure. The impact against the bark momentarily forgotten, he gave in to the sensations coursing through his body. She wasted no time yanking his pants down his hips, exposing his bare ass to the chilly air. Though he hissed momentarily, his concern was quickly overshadowed by the sight before him.

She dropped to her knees and looked up at him, her dark eyes locking with his. Gripping his cock with purpose, she continued to hold his gaze. The image of her on her knees, his dick in her hands, was one that would be etched in his memory forever. With a seductive slide of her tongue along his shaft, she elicited a loud groan from him, causing his eyes to flutter closed momentarily.

Forcing himself to look down at her again, he slipped his hand into her hair, gently pushing it away from her face. He wanted an unobstructed view as she swallowed him whole. The sight of her, with her lips wrapped around him, was undeniably beautiful to watch.

He couldn't believe his luck. He did not know how he had gotten so fortunate, but as he looked down at her worshipping him, he felt like the luckiest man alive. "You are so good at this," he praised her, and she smiled up at him.

She swirled her tongue around the head of his cock before swallowing him whole again.

Suddenly, a booming voice echoed through the trees above them, startling them both. "Fucking Christ."

"Dylan." Blake quickly pulled away from Sam and hastily pulled his sweats up around his hips. He reached down and helped Sam to her feet, putting an arm protectively around her waist.

Dylan, red-faced and hands on his hips, expressed his anger. "You know, I followed you two up here, but I didn't think—Shit!" He paced along the trail, clearly upset. "My sister, you son of a fucking bitch."

Sam stepped forward, trying to reason with her brother. "Dylan, stop. You can't be mad at Blake."

Dylan pointed at Blake, his face filled with anger. "He broke the code. He knows what he did. I specifically told that bastard to stay the hell away from you."

Sam appeared angry. "You aren't my keeper, Dyl. You don't get to have a say about who I'm with."

"Like Casey?" he growled.

Sam shook her head, her face turning red. Blake watched as her demeanor changed. "I'm sick of you trying to control my life. I'm twenty-six years old. Everyone gets to make their own decisions, Dylan, even you!"

He reeled back at her words, then turned his attention to Blake. "I'm done with you," he said firmly. "I told you to stay away from her, so this is your mess. Don't ever speak to me again."

"Dylan, stop," he yelled, as he turned and stormed off down the trail.

Sam growled angrily, "Let him go."

"Dammit!" Blake exclaimed. He knew Dylan would take this badly, but he was pretty sure Dylan catching his little sister sucking Blake's cock was the worst-case scenario. He had no idea how to un-fuck this.

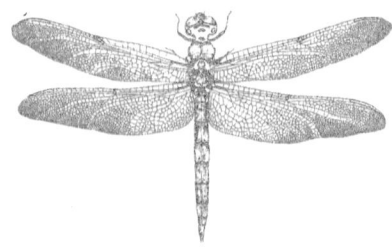

Chapter Thirteen

Samantha

"Do we really have to go through all this bullshit?" Jax growled angrily, gripping the car door as he hovered over the wheelchair beside it. Her brother was nothing if not stubborn, but that stubborn attitude had earned him a quick release from the hospital due to his relentless devotion to his physical therapy. Because of that, the doctors were pleased with his success and felt that he could continue that recovery at home as long as he stayed on top of his exercises and continued with his daily walking.

She pushed the chair closer. "Would you just sit down?" she pleaded with her brother.

"I don't need this damn chair," he grumbled under his breath.

The cool November air blew through the long driveway in front of their family home, carrying with it the falling leaves that left a brown dusting of debris on the ground. "Down you go," she said as she pushed on her brother's shoulder, easing him into the wheelchair.

"Damn, sis. A bit rough for a nursemaid," he said.

She shook her head with a chuckle. "You're out of the hospital now, so no more hot blonde nurses fluffing your pillows or whatever they were doing for you."

"You think that was a pillow they were fluffing?" he said, earning a smack on the back of his head.

She rolled him up the makeshift ramp that her father had built to the front porch, and as the front door opened, Dylan stood in the entrance, staring at her blankly. The awkward silence hung in the air.

"Are we gonna stare at each other, or was freezing to death part of my recovery?" Jax said, breaking the silence.

Dylan finally looked away from her, blinking, and then greeted his brother. "Bout time you got your lazy ass out of bed," Dylan said.

"I missed you too, bro!" Jax said with a smile as she pushed him into the house.

The smell of hamburgers sizzling on the stovetop wafted through the house. "The prodigal son returns," Jax sang happily as he was wheeled through the kitchen.

"Welcome home, son." Their father turned around, staring at his son with a sad smile. "I'm glad there's finally someone else around this house. Maybe you can figure out why these two keep staring daggers at each other," their father said, gesturing to her and Dylan. Jax looked between them with a questioning glance, trying to make sense of the situation.

"I gotta go to the shop," Dylan said dryly, grabbing the keys to the truck and storming out the door.

Jax stared at her, confused and concerned. "What the fuck was that about?" he asked, his voice filled with frustration.

Sam glared angrily, realizing she didn't have the answers she could provide him. Exasperated, she replied, "How should I know?"

Her brother stared at her, clearly unsatisfied with that response. Just then, her phone buzzed in her pocket, and she was grateful for the interruption.

"Saved by the buzz," she muttered, pulling out her phone to find a flurry of texts from Blake.

Blake

> I need your help

Blake

> Somethings wrong with Kelley

Blake

> I got into it with her at work and it was bad

Blake

> she was really shady about something but wont tell me what

Blake

> Then she ran off

Blake

I think she might be at the high school. its
kind of her thing when shes angry.

Blake

Do you think she might talk to you?

As she frowned while reading the messages, she snapped, "Sorry, I need to run out and take care of something really quickly."

Uncomfortably, her father and Jax exchanged glances, an apparent unease of being alone together. Her brother appeared annoyed. "You really have to go out now?"

"Sorry, it can't be helped." She swiftly texted Blake back, informing him she was on her way out.

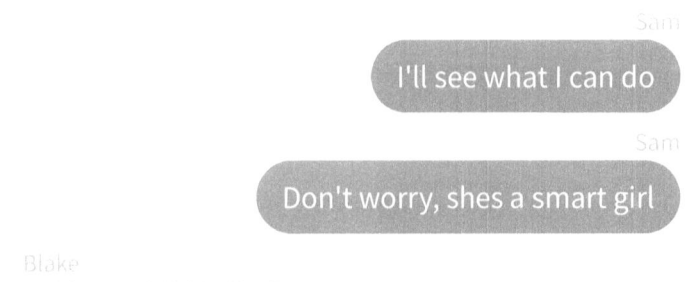

Sam

I'll see what I can do

Sam

Don't worry, shes a smart girl

Blake

Youre the best Sam

Pulling up to the old high school brought back a lot of memories, both good and bad. While there were good memories, like sitting in the stands, watching her brothers and Blake play football on Friday nights. The majority of the memories were not so pleasant. In high school, Sam wasn't popular, and losing her mother at a young age left her feeling vulnerable and alone, especially when it came to understanding anything related to femininity.

She never found girls to be kind; in fact, most of the time they were cruel. She remembered one time in particular, having to borrow a pair of her brother's sweats because she had started her period at school and didn't know who to talk to about it. Unfortunately, everyone made fun of her because the sweats were three sizes too big. Feeling humiliated, she hid in the locker rooms for three classes, waiting until the school had cleared out before going home to avoid the catcalls and harassment from Donna Draper and her friends.

She spent countless gym classes being made fun of when they changed clothes for wearing boy's underwear because her father bought her boxers to wear until she turned sixteen and shopped for her own clothes.

Additionally, her hairstyle was limited to ponytails because her dad wasn't skilled in any other hairstyles. Makeup was also out of the question until after graduation, as her father did not understand it. As a result, she faced whispers and rumors that she must be a lesbian. She didn't date until after graduation due to her awkward nature and overprotective brothers.

To make matters worse, girls started avoiding changing in front of her after Donna, who was a grade below her, spread a false rumor that she had caught Sam staring at her in the shower. High school had been a nightmare for Sam, so being on the grounds again gave her anxiety.

Her phone buzzed beside her, and she checked to see if it was Blake.

Casey

Trying not to get offended

Casey

havent heard from you in weeks

Casey

bed still misses you

Casey

check in if you arent too busy

Casey

at this point you owe me tit pics sweetness

She didn't have time for Casey right now. She clicked her phone off and shoved it in her jacket, pulling her coat tight around her to keep out the chill of the night air.

The lights were on at the football field, prompting her to walk toward the entrance by the gate. As she approached, she noticed movement by the bleachers, accompanied by a puff of smoke and a flash of a colored blazer. It was clear that her arrival was not hidden by the metal bleachers, as she immediately heard a groan of disapproval from the young girl.

"Did my brother send you to spy on me?" the girl asked, her apprehension obvious, considering her disapproving stare.

"That depends," she said, her hair blowing in the chilly breeze. The young girl continued to stare at her, her expression filled with uncertainty. "Does your brother know you smoke those?"

She raised her hand, revealing the cigarette she had been trying to keep hidden, and shrugged. "He would just assume it was drugs and freak out like he does about everything."

"That sounds like Blake, but those things will kill you."

She protested, but realization suddenly washed over her, causing her to open her mouth in horror before stamping out the cigarette with her foot. "Shit, sorry, Sam, I forgot about your mom." Kelley stared down at the extinguished butt of the cigarette and sat quietly.

Sam glanced around the football field, reminiscing about the last time she had been there. It felt like ages ago, and high school seemed so inconsequential now. "You want to tell me what's going on?" Sam asked. "Blake said you guys got into it."

Kelley sighed beside her. "Do you know what it's like growing up with boy wonder?" Her tone was not angry but conveyed a sense of inadequacy. "Blake never does anything wrong. He runs the diner, helping Mom with everything. Hell, he's raised me since I was five years old. How does anyone live up to something like that?"

"No one is asking you to be Blake," Sam said sincerely.

Kelley shook her head. "Did you know he gave up culinary school in New York?" Sam, of course, knew this, but she was surprised that Kelley was aware as well. "And before you ask, he doesn't know I know. I found the scholarship in his room one day when I was looking for porn." Sam tried not to appear shocked. "But the point is, he threw away something he's dreamed about for years to take care of us. That's a Goddamn saint. And all I do is complain and get in the way."

Sam studied Kelley before responding, "How do you think you get in the way? Blake says you are a tremendous help at the diner."

Kelley laughed loudly as she replied, "He only says that because he has no other help. But he knows I hate it there. I don't want to work at the diner every single day."

Sam furrowed her brow, intrigued. "And you think he does?"

Kelley bit her lip. "Honestly, I don't think Blake wants to be in Titusville at all. He's here, out of duty. I think if Dad were still alive, Blake would have taken the scholarship and run years ago." Sam nodded, sharing the same suspicion. "I don't want to be stuck here like he is. But I don't know how to say that without sounding like a real asshole, and it's not fair to him if I get out and he doesn't."

Sam asked, "What do you want to do?"

Kelley, sitting on her hands and rocking back and forth, replied, "I might have applied to the nursing program at Berkeley College and got accepted."

Sam wasn't usually surprised by someone, but this time, she was. "Kelley, are you serious? That's amazing news. Why haven't you told anyone? That's quite an accomplishment."

With a shrug, Kelley stated firmly, "Because I'm not going."

Sam sighed. "What is it with you Forresters and giving up great opportunities?"

"I can't go if Blake stays," Kelley said, "and Blake won't leave Mom. So, there isn't anything either of us can do except stay." Kelley sighed, while Sam could only shake her head in response.

"I just wonder," Sam said, "if perhaps you both are leaving one important person out of these discussions." Kelley stared at Sam in confusion. "Don't you think your mom might want to weigh in on her opinion? You are both deciding for her based on how you think she would feel."

"It's just easier when we don't add more to her plate." Kelley stared off toward the other end of the field. "She has had enough to worry about since Dad died."

"Kelley, that was thirteen years ago. Maybe your mom is stronger than you guys realize," Sam said with a light raise of her shoulder.

Kelley seemed to think about Sam's words and then gazed off toward the other side of the field, lost in her thoughts. "I just don't know if Mom can handle the diner if we both leave, and I'd hate to disappoint Blake by leaving him to deal with all of this on his own."

"It sounds like you are taking on a lot of worry and responsibility for one person. Besides, I hardly think you could ever disappoint your brother. I think maybe you need to start worrying about what *you* want out of your life and let Blake and your mom take care of themselves," she said honestly.

Kelley suddenly redirected the conversation, turning to face Sam with a playful grin. "If you're so smart, what are you doing with my brother?"

Sam simply shook her head, amused by the question. "You know," Sam reminisced, "when I went to school here, I thought he was the hottest guy in class."

Kelley made a disgusted face. "Gross." She scrunched her nose. "I don't know how he managed to swing a hot chick like you."

Blushing at the compliment, Sam responded, "Trust me, he's had hotter."

"If you mean Double D, she's trash." Kelley's voice dripped with disdain and anger. "Girls like her are full of hate and fear. They despise other girls that aren't like them. Women shouldn't tear other women down."

Sam nodded in agreement, acknowledging the reality of the situation. "Unfortunately, I didn't find a lot of girls like you when I was in high school."

Kelley chuckled. "I'm not like other girls, and they don't exist here either." A hint of sadness entered her voice. "Most of the time, I have to hide who I am. The guys, they don't understand me, or they tell me I'm just going through a phase. Or worse, the ones who get excited because they want to watch." Sam listened, empathizing with Kelley's struggle. "But the girls, well, the girls are the worst. They are either intimidated by me or hate me. And if I'm lucky enough to find a gay woman in this town, then I'm not gay enough for them or I need to pick a side."

"I'm sorry you've had to deal with that," Sam said, her voice sincere as she wrapped an arm around the girl's back. Kelley wiped away an errant tear. "I can't say I understand where you are coming from. I've always been straight. However, growing up, people spread rumors about me because I was different. I was raised by my dad and my brothers, and I didn't have a mother's touch. Everyone looked at me differently here." She sighed. "I can tell you it got better when I moved to the city. But there will always be people who look at you differently, who judge you. This world isn't a kind place."

"Ain't that the fucking truth," the girl chimed in.

Sam nodded in agreement. "But you have people who love you, who support you for who you are, no matter who that is. Your mom, Blake, and the Lancasters will always be in your corner." Kelley leaned over and wrapped her arms around her, hugging her tightly.

Kelley then teased, "If my dipshit brother ever does anything stupid, just know that I like women."

Sam shook her head and laughed. "How about I get you home?"

Chapter Fourteen

Blake

Blake's confrontation with his sister that evening was worse than their usual arguments. Earlier that day, Kelley had seemed out of sorts when she arrived for her shift. However, as the day went on, her mood only worsened. Every time Blake asked her to do something, it seemed like she took it as an insult. Eventually, their exchange escalated into an all-out battle of wits at the counter in front of a customer.

Feeling the tension, Blake suggested that Kelley take a break to compose herself. But instead of taking his advice, she lashed out at him, saying that not everyone could be as perfect as him. Her comment caught him off guard. In reality, he knew he wasn't perfect. Lately, he had been making more mistakes than ever before. From mishandling the diner orders to his complicated relationship with Dylan, and his confusion about what he was doing with Sam, Blake felt like a walking, talking mess.

Realizing he needed to clear his mind, Blake knew he had to talk to Dylan. It had been ages since they last spoke, and the silence between them was unbearable. Walking into Boondock's bar, he scanned the room in search of his friend. Finally, he spotted Dylan at the back, aimlessly slinging darts at the board. Taking a deep breath, Blake extended an olive branch by ordering a couple of beers, hoping it would serve as a peace offering and prevent any darts from being aimed in his direction.

"You know," Blake joked as he sat the beer on the tall table next to the dartboard, "you used to tell me darts were for losers or guys who couldn't play pool." Dylan aimed a dart over Blake's shoulder and tossed it toward the board, causing Blake to flinch as it hit the wall behind him.

"Did you come here to tell me it's over between you and my sister?" Dylan said in a strained voice. "Because if you are here for any other reason, I still owe you a punch in the fucking face after the scene I walked into out in those woods."

Blake swallowed hard. "I know you're pissed."

Dylan's face turned red, anger forming on his lips as he took a step toward Blake. "Pissed? Pissed doesn't begin to cover it, Blake," he said angrily. "I told you to stay the hell away from her, and then you went and took advantage of her, anyway."

"That's not at all what happened," Blake argued, trying to defend himself. In frustration, Dylan shoved Blake against his shoulder.

"You couldn't go get your dick sucked from your goddamn girlfriend. You had to pick my little sister," Dylan shouted, his voice filled with rage.

"I don't have a girlfriend," Blake shouted back, squaring his shoulders to face him. "I told you we broke up."

Confused by the escalating tension, Donna Draper stepped between the two of them, placing her hands against Blake's chest as she pressed herself against him. "What is going on with you two?" she asked, her voice filled with concern. "Blake, baby, why are you fighting with Dylan?"

"Don't call me baby." Blake scowled, stepping away from her. "And stay out of this, Donna. It's none of your business."

Dylan glared at Blake while Donna stood between them, creating tension in the air. "Just leave, Donna," Dylan warned, the frustration becoming palpable.

"Don't tell me what to do, Dylan. You've already disappointed me enough in this situation." Donna chastised Dylan.

As Blake observed the interaction, curiosity filled his eyes. He wondered what they were talking about. Dylan stepped back, stumbling slightly as he slurred his words. "Go to hell, Don...Donna. I'm sick of you threatening me," he said. Regret laced his words as he added, "I never should have met you that night."

Blake, unable to contain his impatience and growing anger, interrupted them. "What night?" he asked quietly.

Dylan's expression changed, his face paling, before scoffing loudly. "You know what? Screw this," he said, shaking his head at Donna.

Donna shrugged nonchalantly, as her tone with Dylan took on a teasing yet threatening vibe. "Oh, come on, Dilly. Do you want to tell him, or should I?"

Blake's patience was wearing thin. "Tell me what?"

Donna smiled at Dylan and then placed a comforting hand on his chest. "That night you and I got into that big fight about our future a few months back—" Blake's memory resurfaced. He remembered the argument, the anger radiating from Donna when he expressed his decision not to move out of town with her. The fight had escalated, and Donna's behavior had become obnoxious. Blake had simply wanted to have a beer and forget about it, while Donna had wanted to fuck and make up.

"Get to the point, Donna," Blake said, annoyed.

She giggled airily before revealing, "Even though you had no interest in me that night, someone else did."

"Shut the hell up, Donna." Dylan's anger flared, and he clenched his teeth.

Blake's gaze met his friend's, now filled with a sense of betrayal. Shocked, Blake confronted Dylan, struggling to believe what he was hearing. After all the talk about bro-code and the accusations of breaking it with his sister, he couldn't fathom that Dylan would do this. "You had sex with my girlfriend?" Blake's voice quivered with disbelief and hurt.

Dylan, his regret palpable, spoke quietly, barely audible. "I was drunk. I hardly remember it."

"You hypocrite," Blake said loudly. "Girlfriends are part of the bro-code, too."

Dylan's voice rose as he stepped toward him. "You fucked my sister."

The tension in the air grew thicker as Blake yelled, his face red with anger. He lunged toward Dylan, wrapping his arms around his friend's waist, and the two of them crashed to the ground with a thud.

Dylan quickly gained the upper hand, rolling on top of Blake and delivering a powerful punch to his cheek with a loud crack. Blake, defending himself, raising his arms in front of his face to block the next blow. Amid the chaos, he lifted his knee into Dylan's stomach, causing him to roll onto his side. Taking advantage of the moment, Blake struck Dylan's eye with a punch, feeling the pain in his knuckles as they connected with bone.

Suddenly, a pair of firm hands gripped Blake's arms and pulled him off his friend, while another man yanked Dylan away simultaneously. Behind him, Rusty's gravelly voice broke through the commotion. "That will be enough of that, you two. Time for you to go home."

Blake sat on his front porch, holding a frozen bag of peas against his cheek. He knew that the injury would leave a mark in the morning. Earlier, he and Dylan had silently gone their separate ways at Boondock's. Honestly, even if Blake had years to think about it, he wouldn't have known what to say to Dylan. The knowledge of Dylan's betrayal, sleeping with Donna while they were still together, had hurt him deeply.

It wasn't just Dylan that he blamed, though; he understood Donna was manipulative. He just never expected that she would use his best friend against him. Perhaps he had been too gullible.

Suddenly, a pair of headlights turned up his driveway, illuminating the porch and his face. His sister sat in the passenger seat of Sam's VW bug, laughing at something they were discussing.

He recognized the moment they noticed him sitting there, sensing that something was wrong. Sam hurried up the porch steps and kneeled at his feet, concerned. "What happened to you?" she asked.

He chuckled, feeling the pain intensify as he groaned and pressed the cold vegetables against his throbbing cheek. "Would you believe me if I said I walked into a door?"

"No, not at all," she said, annoyance in her voice.

He sighed as her fingers gently traced the bruise on his cheek. "I went to talk to Dylan."

"And this was your idea of talking?" she said sarcastically.

"It wasn't the plan, no," he said with a sigh, noticing his sister Kelley standing against the door watching them. Concerned, he asked her, "You okay?"

She responded with a smile, "Doing better than your face, loser." Despite the pain, he appreciated her humor in that moment and tried to smile. "I'm going to bed. Goodnight, you two," Kelley sang mischievously.

Once they were alone, Sam sighed as she examined his face. "Now, do you want to tell me what really happened?"

He shook his head. "Does it really matter?" He pointed to his face. "We have matching bruises, there was some shouting, and we are even further from reconciling than we were before I walked in the damn bar."

Overwhelmed, guilt spread on her face, Sam groaned sadly. "Oh, Blake, this is all my fault."

He reassured her by grabbing her hand from his cheek and holding it in his lap. "Stop. This is between Dylan and me, and not all of this gorgeous makeover had to do with you tonight." He chuckled.

Her lips pinched tightly. "Does it hurt?"

Wincing, he replied, "Like a son of a bitch." Then, with a hint of vulnerability, he asked, "Does that make me less of a man?"

"I think it's sexy," she said, placing a kiss on his forehead.

He chuckled, feeling a pinch of pain, and admitted, "I'll take sexy."

She examined his hands, which were still covered in blood. "Come on, let's get you cleaned up."

Pulling him up by his hand, she led him into the house. As they walked, he whispered, "You know, I might have bruises elsewhere," pulling her closer to his chest and smiling down at her.

"Oh, really?" she said with a playful smile. "Well, I wouldn't want you to go to bed without a full checkup."

He wet a washcloth and gathered some supplies from under the sink, including a first aid kit. "Everyone's asleep. We should, uh,

take this somewhere more private," he said. She giggled as he guided her quietly through the house, sneaking toward his bedroom.

Chapter Fifteen

Samantha

I'm so sorry to do this on your first night home

Emergency came up I have to take care of

dont wait up for me

But I promise tomorrow my focus is on you

youre leaving me with dad on my first night!!!!!!!!!!

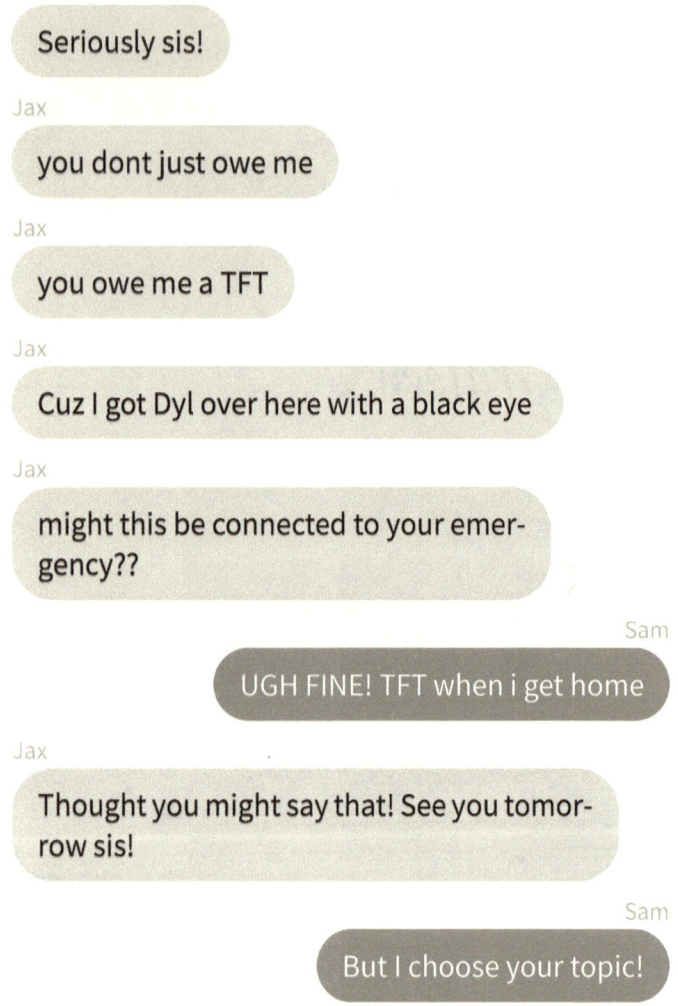

Jax
Seriously sis!

Jax
you dont just owe me

Jax
you owe me a TFT

Jax
Cuz I got Dyl over here with a black eye

Jax
might this be connected to your emergency??

Sam
UGH FINE! TFT when i get home

Jax
Thought you might say that! See you tomorrow sis!

Sam
But I choose your topic!

Samantha groaned as she finished her text with Jax. Tonight was going to cost her a truth for a truth with her brother. She knew she had to make his truth worth her while because she would have to explain to him where she was tonight in hers.

Setting her phone on Blake's desk, she took a moment to look around the room. In all the time she had known him, she had never been up here. This was the holy grail of bedrooms for teenage Samantha. She used to lie in bed and imagine what his room looked like.

Running her fingers along the row of books that lined his shelves, she noticed an array of cooking books, a vast collection of Stephen King novels, and the entire set of hardback Harry Potter books. On the top shelf, there was a photo of Blake and Dylan in their football jerseys from their senior year of high school. She remembered taking the picture the night of their senior home-coming game.

His dresser contained various trophies from school and trinkets he must have collected over the years. There was also a small box with the initials R.F. on it, which she assumed belonged to his late father.

Surprisingly, attached to the mirror was her own face looking back at her. It was a picture from her high school graduation, where she was standing on the football field in her cap and gown with Blake's arm around her shoulder. The sun was at their back as they both smiled at the camera. The picture was jammed behind other photos, as if it had been there for years.

"That's one of my favorites." She jumped when Blake entered the room.

"I didn't know you still had it." Turning toward him, she smiled back and walked over to take the washcloth from him, gesturing for him to sit on the bed. She brushed his cheek, cleaning the blood and dirt from his face as he looked up at her.

Settling between his legs, his hands wrapped around her waist. He rocked her lightly in his arms as she brushed the hair off his forehead. "I may not have realized you were an option for me back then, but you were always special to me."

"You were untouchable," she whispered, her longing for him clear in the way she stared at him. "I wanted you so badly all the time. I wanted you to see me."

Her fingers gently traced the bruise on his cheek, and he responded by grasping her hand, holding it firm against his face. "Does this feel untouchable, Sam?" he asked, his voice filled with vulnerability. She sighed softly as he brought her hands to his mouth, delicately grazing his lips against each knuckle. The gesture was slow, methodical, and undeniably erotic. "I see you now," he said softly, his words filled with newfound understanding.

She kissed his forehead, then pulled away, looking down at him. "I should go."

She felt his grip around her tighten, unwilling to let her leave. "Stay," he pleaded softly.

She shook her head, aware of the potential consequences. "I shouldn't. Your mom might see me, and you're in no condition for—"

Before she could finish her sentence, he interrupted her, his hand sliding to the back of her neck, pulling her mouth down to his in a passionate kiss. His lips were soft, his tongue teasingly slipping across her own. "So be gentle with me, Lancaster," he murmured, his voice filled with desire.

"Blake—" she started to protest as he interrupted her.

"Sam, come on. You can leave before Mom gets up, and I believe there was a certain fantasy you thought I might be able to help you with." His hands slid down to her ass, gently squeezing, a mischievous glint in his eyes.

"Oh, yeah?" She raised a brow, intrigued. He stood up, making his way toward his dresser, opening the bottom drawer and rummaging through it. When he turned back, he was holding something in his hand. With a smirk, he tossed it to her. She caught it, pulling it away from her face, reading the words "Forrester" and the number eighteen on the back. It was his high school football jersey.

He clicked on his phone, and as the song "Crush" by Cigarettes after Sex started playing, she immediately recognized it from the countless times she had played it while thinking about Blake. With the music filling the room, he walked closer to her. "Gonna have to be quiet, Sam." He smirked. "I'm not sure how thin these walls are." He reached down and pulled on the bottom of his shirt, lifting it over his head. "I've never actually tested the bed, either."

She swallowed nervously. "You've never had sex in here before?"

He shook his head, unbuttoning his pants. "You ever know any other losers my age that still live at home?" He laughed sarcastically. "Really ruins the sex life."

"Dylan still lives at home," she said, quickly reminding him of another loveable loser she knew.

He shook his head. "Dylan lives in an apartment over your garage with his own entrance. His loser status is slightly above mine." With that, he discarded his pants, and his boxers quickly followed.

He walked over to his bed, lying down and propping his hand behind his head as he watched her. "Your move, Lancaster."

Sam lifted her shirt over her head, dropping it to her feet. She shimmied out of her pants, leaving her in her bra and panties. She reached behind her back, unhooking her bra and dropping it to the ground as Blake slid his hand onto his semi-erect cock, watching her intently.

She slipped the jersey over her head, immediately losing herself in the overwhelming scent of Blake. The oversized shirt engulfed her, falling around her mid-thigh. She hooked her fingers in her panties and slid them down her legs, stepping out of them. "Like what you see, big boy?" she purred while he stroked himself, grinning.

"Why don't you come find out!" he dared her.

With confidence, she sauntered toward the bed, her fingers gently touching his knee, sliding slowly up his thigh as she approached him.

She climbed onto the bed, straddling him and purring with desire. "Okay, big boy, why don't you let me take care of you?"

Gripping her thighs tightly under the jersey, he held on so firmly that she knew she would have bruises in the morning. Brushing her wet center along his shaft, she bit her lip to keep herself from moaning. Blake cursed under his breath as he watched her intently.

She playfully hushed him. "You have to be quiet, baby." His moans grew even louder, prompting her to lean over and press her mouth against his, silencing him. Sitting back up, she ran her fingers down his chest until she reached his hardened cock, pumping him in her hand while watching his face burn with desire.

Lifting herself up, she positioned herself above him, sinking down onto him with a quiet murmur. Blake's hands roamed her stomach under the jersey, sliding up to her breasts as she rocked her hips against him. With each bounce, she felt his hips lift, thrusting up into her.

The bed squeaked beneath them, its sound reverberating throughout the small room. Reaching down, she pulled Blake up to her, their mouths colliding in a clash of heat and desire. This was more than just a kiss; it was a moment when two hearts beat to the same rhythm.

As she fell over the edge that night, panting against his mouth, he wrapped his arms around her, pulling her close to his body.

His gentleness and honesty as he whispered her name against her neck while drifting off to sleep conveyed a truth that she had been running from. It was a truth she knew she wasn't ready to face.

She was in love with Blake Forrester, and it terrified her.

The sunlight tickled her nose as she rolled over, and it was then that she first noticed the feeling of being restricted to her spot in the bed. She pinched her eyes tightly before slowly peering through them at the unfamiliar surroundings. After a moment, she felt his arm around her midsection and heard the soft sound of his breathing in her ear. She had stayed at Blake's last night, and the memories of the night before brought a warm smile to her face as she remembered drifting off to sleep in his arms.

Everything had felt so perfect. However, she couldn't help but wish things could be different. She didn't live in Titusville and had no plans to move back home. Blake, on the other hand, was dedicated to his mother and the diner, and nothing was going to change that for him. As much as she was discovering newfound feelings, she needed to remember that this was only temporary and that their relationship couldn't work.

Not wanting to deal with reality this early in the morning, she tried to erase the thoughts from her mind. She rolled out from under his arm, trying not to wake him as she slid quietly out of bed. She couldn't help as she watched him sleep to notice that he slept like a restless boy, with his leg adrift on top of the blanket, his hair sticking out in unruly yet sexy ways that made her want to crawl back in bed and run her fingers through each silken strand. He was the most gorgeous man she had ever laid eyes on.

She didn't have experience with many men, but she couldn't help but compare him to Casey. Unlike Casey Anderson, whose frame was fit and hard in all the right places, with tight muscles from playing ball day and night, Blake's body was softer. Though his features may be more down to earth, they were nothing to scoff at either. Years of playing football had kept him healthy, and riding his bike every day definitely kept his muscles toned.

But it was Blake's kind and gentle face that had always attracted her to him. His eyes had a way of drawing you in, as if they were peering directly into your soul. No one had ever consumed her so completely, leaving her in a constant state of restless euphoria. However, Sam refused to let her emotions control her. Sex, for her, was about pleasure on her own terms, not something that should overpower her ability to think. Despite this, everything about Blake Forrester left her confused.

Quietly, she gathered her clothing and slipped on her pants, shoving her undergarments into her bag. She put her jacket on over Blake's Jersey.

Can't blame a girl for wanting a souvenir. Maybe she would remember to return it before leaving for Pittsburgh. Maybe not.

Standing over his peacefully sleeping form, she bent over and placed her lips softly on his forehead before tiptoeing out of the room.

Getting down the stairs was easy enough in the quiet old house, but the wooden floors seemed to creak and moan with every step, as if the house itself was a nosy old grandma just dying to tell her secrets to her quilt circle.

"Would you like some breakfast before you sneak off?" Startled by the sound of Blake's mother's voice, Sam jumped and instinctively clutched her chest. She turned to find the woman standing at the kitchen island, holding a cup of coffee and wearing a smile on her face.

"Mrs. F, I'm sorry. I...I, uh, I thought everyone was in bed," Sam stammered, her cheeks flushing with embarrassment.

The woman poured out a cup of coffee, then slid it across the wooden counter toward Sam. "I like to get up early and catch the sunrise." Reluctantly, Sam walked into the kitchen and accepted the cup of coffee, biting her lip as a heavy awkwardness settled between them. "You don't have to be embarrassed, Sam. Blake's a good kid, but I always forget that he's not actually a kid." Mrs. Forrester gave Sam a sly smile. "He sacrifices a lot to still live at home with his mom and take care of everything he does around here."

Sam buried her hands in her face. "I'm still mortified," she admitted, laughing nervously.

Mrs. Forrester chuckled. "Just be happy it was me and not your father," she said, raising her brow playfully. "Not sure Ken is ready to catch his baby girl with a man yet. Fathers take a lot longer to be okay with that sort of thing."

Sam mumbled, "And brothers."

Mrs. Forrester nodded in understanding. "I'm guessing Dylan doesn't approve."

Sam shook her head and frowned. "More like, despises the entire thing."

"Boys have a tendency to work things out in their own way," Mrs. Forrester said, taking a sip of her coffee. Sam didn't have the heart to tell her it wouldn't matter anyway once she went back to Pittsburgh. Changing the topic, Mrs. Forrester asked, "So, how's your brother doing?"

Sam was relieved at the change in conversation. "He actually came home last night from the hospital," she said, snickering. "He's crankier than I've ever seen him, but that's Jax for you. He could be irritable at a county fair with a cold glass of beer."

They shared a laugh, and then she made a soft sound before asking, "And how is your father doing with Jax?" Surprised by the question, she was also intrigued to think that maybe Mrs. Forrester knew more about what was going on with her father than she thought.

Sam replied cautiously, "Strained for some reason," watching Mrs. Forrester's reaction.

Mrs. Forrester laughed as if remembering something. "You know, your dad once got caught sneaking out of my bedroom window when we were in high school." She shook her head. "Second floor. He had to climb the trellis." Blake's mom sighed and smiled softly.

"My dad did physical labor. He must have really liked you." Sam smiled sadly; it was odd hearing a story about her dad being with anyone other than her mother.

"God, we were crazy about each other. He was the love of my life," she said with a chuckle. "Bobby will always be my soul mate, but your dad and I, we were restless spirits."

"My dad? Restless." Sam found it hard to believe that her dad was restless. He had always appeared so settled.

She bit her lip and laughed softly. "We used to talk about buying an RV and taking it across America, just exploring the world for what it offered."

"My dad hasn't even left the state. Are you sure we are talking about the same person?" Sam asked.

Mrs. Forrester nodded and stared into her coffee cup. "Oh, this was way before your mom. After he fell in love with Mary, everything changed for him." She picked up her cup and walked it over to the sink. "Your mom was his entire world. He would do anything for her. And once Jax came around, well, I think he just found a new dream."

Sam softly mumbled, "He's so distracted lately," not even sure if she meant to say it.

Mrs. Forrester stared at her, searching for the right words. Finally, she said, "I won't betray your dad's trust, Sam. So, you'll need to talk to him directly, but—" Once again, she seemed to be looking for the words, and Sam realized that Blake's mom knew exactly what was going on with her dad. "For years, your dad has had a hard time letting go of your mom."

Sam shook her head in disagreement. "Not Dad. He told us when she passed that death is just a part of life, and once that part passes, you move on. Dad let Mom go a long time ago."

At this, Mrs. Forrester actually laughed loudly. "Oh, Ken!" she said, mostly to herself. Then she continued, "Honey, I'm going to tell you something, and I need you not to judge me."

Sam shook her head before responding, "I can't imagine I would ever judge you."

"You know your dad and I get together every year to celebrate Bobby and Mary." Sam nodded, fully aware of the close bond the couples had shared before their respective partners passed away. "A few years back, your dad and I got together to celebrate, and I think maybe we had too much wine because I just remember laughing harder than I had in years, though it could have been your dad's jokes, he is quite hilarious when he wants to be." Sam couldn't really imagine her dad being *that* funny. "Well, one glass led to another, and too many glasses led to me kissing your father," Mrs. Forrester confessed.

Samantha's mouth dropped open, her eyes widening in astonishment. "Wait, you...you and Dad?" she stuttered.

"Don't forget, we dated for four years," Mrs. Forrester said with a laugh, slightly amused.

"Yeah, but still...gross." Sam's face crinkled in disgust. "I'm sorry, I just never saw that coming."

Trying to ease the tension, Mrs. Forrester smiled sincerely and reached across the table to touch Sam's hand. "Your dad had a similar reaction," she admitted sadly. "I think I'll always love your father, but he's unable to let go of the memory of your mother." Sam's confusion deepened as she frowned, contemplating everything her father had taught her over the years about suppressing emotions and moving on from the past. "And I think this town holds too many painful memories," Mrs. Forrester said, hoping to shed some light on her previous statement.

"I don't understand." Sam shook her head, feeling lost.

Sensing her confusion, Mrs. Forrester patted her hand reassuringly. "Sweetie, talk to your dad about it," she said. She stood and picked up Sam's empty cup and walked over to the sink. "And don't forget to let him know that I'm expecting all of you for Thanksgiving dinner this year."

Sam managed to smile and wrapped her coat around her, nodding before heading outside toward her car, unsure about how to process everything she had just learned.

Chapter Sixteen

Blake

When Blake woke up, he discovered that his bed was empty, no longer occupied with the dark curly hair that had taken over his pillow the previous night. He had spent hours lying awake last night, watching her sleep, determined not to close his eyes so that he could steal just one more glimpse of her face while she lay in his arms.

Eventually, sleep had claimed him, but now he found himself alone, with only the lingering scent of her perfume as a reminder of her presence. As he stretched his arms and let out a loud yawn, he sat up and surveyed his room. Glancing at the time on his clock, he realized that he still had an hour before he needed to leave for work.

Climbing out of bed, he walked past the mirror, pausing to examine the dark bruising on his cheek. There was a gash under his eye, and he couldn't help but be impressed at how well Sam had cleaned up the cut. As he reached up to touch his chin, he winced at the sight of the red splotches on his knuckles. Closing his eyes, he took a deep breath, trying to push aside thoughts of Dylan's betrayal. It was difficult for him to comprehend how things had gotten this bad between him and his best friend.

He had met Dylan when they were both just four years old, while their mothers were busy shopping for groceries. They had exchanged gummy bears while patiently waiting for their mothers to finish their conversation about something neither of them could possibly remember.

From that moment on, they were inseparable, thick as thieves. Not once did they exchange an angry word growing up. The most heated argument they ever had was during a high school football game when one of them ran a play incorrectly. But now, it felt as if everything had fallen apart.

He dressed for his day at work and left his room in search of breakfast, surprised to follow the smell of bacon to the kitchen. When he reached his destination, he found his mother dishing out eggs and bacon onto a plate. "I figured you might want some protein before work," she said.

"Mom, you didn't have to do this," he said, kissing her cheek and taking a plate from her. He sat down at the table as she smiled and sat down beside him.

"I know I didn't, but it looks like you had a rough night." She pointed to his face. "At least Sam seems to have patched you up well." His heart froze as he stared down at his plate. "She and I had a lovely conversation this morning."

Shit.

"Oh, I uh—she um, well, I didn't um..." he stuttered, unsure of what he was trying to say.

His mother shook her head. "You better be good to that one. She's a keeper."

"I know, Mom, but it's complicated," he said with a sigh.

His mother only nodded and patted him on the hand. "It always is."

Not looking up from his plate, he tentatively asked, "How did you know you were in love with Dad?" His mother chuckled, causing Blake's nose to crinkle and his eyes to roll.

It was typical of his mom to try to lighten the mood when he was grappling with what felt like the biggest hurdle he had ever faced. "You might find my answer too simple," she said, looking into his eyes as he looked up.

"Simple?" he asked.

"He chose me, even when it wasn't easy," she said, narrowing her eyes. "And believe me, it wasn't easy. Ken and your dad, they were inseparable." Blake's thoughts drifted to Dylan and his own dilemma with Sam. "I never cared about having two boys fighting over me, and Lord, did they fight! But Bobby and I, the moment that man looked at me, it was over."

"So, he looked at you and you knew?" he said with a laugh, though sometimes he wondered if his entire world didn't stop the moment Sam looked at him.

She shook her head. "Not quite that simple, but—when I was with him, I felt like I could do anything," she said, smiling and touching his hand. "With your dad, I felt like I was writing a story in a romance novel, and no matter what happened, he was always going to make sure we got our happy ending."

Blake frowned and pulled his hand away. "I don't know what kind of romance novels you are reading, but I think this one got messed up."

"Blake Forrester, don't you ever say that again," his mother scolded. "Your father gave me the best story ever. He gave me my diner, the greatest love story of my life, and the two most beautiful children I could ever ask for."

"And then he left you alone," he said in a mournful tone.

"I'm never alone," she said, touching her hand to her heart. "He's with me, always."

Kelley arrived at the diner and entered the office. The first thing out of her mouth was an insult tossed his way. "You look like shit."

Startled, Blake dropped his glasses onto his desk and looked up at her. He replied sarcastically, "Gee, thanks, Kels."

As she shut the door behind her, enclosing them in the office, Kelley didn't waste any time bringing up the topic on her mind. "So, what's going on with you and Sam?" she asked.

Blake questioned, "Going on?"

Kelley shrugged. "Yes, you obviously like her, and she's into you for some dumbass up reason."

"For some *dumbass* reason?" he said, laughing, clearly noticing that his entire family seemed intent on getting into his business that day.

"Obviously!" she said with a shrug, before asking, "So, are you in love with her or not?"

It was definitely the three million-dollar-question of the day! "I don't really see how that's any of your business," he said.

"Chicks before dicks. That's how it's my business. I like Sam. I'd hate to see her get hurt," Kelley said firmly, crossing her arms and glaring at him. "Especially by my own flesh and blood."

Staring at his sister, he chuckled. "You know, I'm the reason you got to have that little bonding moment with Sam the other night. Does that not grant me any loyalty?"

"That depends. Do you have feelings for her, or are you just using Sam for sex until she goes home?" Blake flinched at the crassness of her question, insulted that his sister would even assume he could do that. He truly cared about Sam in a way he hadn't cared about a woman before, a realization that hit him harder than he expected. Swallowing hard, he locked eyes with his sister as she pressed on. "Well, what exactly are your intentions with Sam Lancaster?"

Chuckling, Blake responded, "It's not that simple. Sam lives in Pitt, and I live here, you know that."

Kelley nodded her head. "You know you don't have to stay here. I know you have other options."

"What are you talking about?" he said with a sigh, clearly not having time for his sister's antics.

"I know about your scholarship," she said, putting her hand on the paperwork in front of him and abruptly halting his work. "I know you are giving up your chance at a real future."

Frustrated, he shook his head and responded, "Kels, I don't have time for this. You know why I can't go." Angrily, he added, "How did you even find out about that?"

She casually shrugged. "I was looking for porn in your room and found your letter."

Shocked, he exclaimed, "What the hell?!"

She ignored his outburst. "Anyway, I think you should consider it. You're made for bigger things, Blake."

He dismissed her comment. "I don't deserve any more of an opportunity than you, sis."

With a passionate wave of her hand, she responded, "Exactly! And I want to go to Berkeley."

Confused, he shook his head and stared at her. "What the hell are you talking about?"

She held his gaze and revealed, "I got into Berkeley's nursing program."

Overwhelmed with pride, he stood up and pulled her into a hug. "Kelley, that's—that's amazing."

However, she frowned, as she firmly expressed an opinion that gave no room for argument. "No, I'm not going unless you take your opportunity. You have sacrificed everything for this family."

"I've done what was required of me, Kels. You would have done the same," he said, sitting back down at his desk. He placed his glasses back on his face and punched a few keys on the keyboard to bring it back to life.

However, his sister made a few disgruntled sounds before yanking the office door open. "You know that's not true, but maybe you're too afraid to do anything else," she said. Before he could argue with her, she was gone, leaving him alone in the quiet office.

Chapter Seventeen

Samantha

As Sam's mind wandered through her conversation with Blake's mom on her short drive back home, she tried to piece together everything she had said about her father. She wanted to combine it with the information she and Dylan had gathered since the accident. Perhaps her conversation with Jax would provide the missing piece of the puzzle she needed before speaking to her dad.

To her surprise, when she pulled into the driveway, her brother was sitting in his wheelchair on the front porch with a cup of coffee, his dog Whiskey lying at his feet. She hadn't expected him to be waiting for her. Walking up the drive, she awkwardly tugged her jacket around her chest. The sound of her feet on the wooden steps caused Whiskey to jump up and rush toward her. She patted his head while her brother smirked at her from across the porch.

With a grin, he shook his head. "Never thought I'd see the day my little sister did the walk of shame."

She groaned, "Who said I was ashamed?"

He chuckled in amusement. "Finally bagged Forrester, huh?"

Her eyes widened in shock as she exclaimed, "Jax!"

He grinned into his coffee cup. "Coming home in his old football jersey was a choice. I'm guessing this explains Dylan's black eye."

With a sigh, she walked over to the chair next to him and plopped down into it with a grunt. "I suppose I owe you my truth," she said.

He grunted. "I feel like I missed a lot lying in that hospital bed."

"Blake and I just...happened..." she said hesitantly, her voice trailing off.

He snorted dismissively. "As if you haven't been making doe eyes at that man since his acne-ridden, sexually awkward high school days." Shaking his head, he added, "Honestly, I can't believe it took him this long to see my little sister as worthy of his time."

She frowned. "Tell that to Dylan."

He turned toward her awkwardly. "Is that why his face looks like roadkill? That damn bro-code crap?" Disgust contorted his face. "They're not kids anymore. He needs to stop acting like he's your keeper."

"I don't think it was just about me," she sadly admitted. "Blake wouldn't tell me the whole story, just that *I* wasn't the only factor." She sighed. "Not that it really matters, anyway. Blake and I are only temporary."

Now her brother directed his annoyance toward her. "What the hell are you talking about now, sis?"

"In case you forgot, I live in Pittsburgh," she said.

"Don't city folks have phones in Pittsburgh? I thought you sophisticated people were better than us small-town folk," he grumbled.

She bit into the nailbed of her finger and stared at the ground. "I'm too old for a long-distance thing. It's not what I'm interested in. Besides, Blake's never going to leave this place."

"I never thought you were the hit-and-run type, Sam," he said, earning a glare from her. Of all the people to lecture her about relationships, he was the last on her list. Jax hadn't had a long-term relationship in—well, ever, for that matter.

"Are you really going to lecture me on relationships?" she challenged him.

He started to respond but then grunted, sinking down into his chair, admitting defeat. "Fine, I just think Blake is a good guy."

"So do I," she said, closing the door on the conversation about Blake. She looked up as a car passed by on the road beyond their driveway. "So, I've given you my truth."

He grumbled and shifted in his seat. "Yeah, I know. But do your job first. I want to walk." Pushing with his hands on the rails of his chair, he scooted to the edge of his seat and placed his feet on the porch. "I'm sick of being in this damn thing."

She was amazed by the stubbornness and sheer will of her brother. The doctor had expected his injury to take longer to heal, and that he might not walk as soon as he did. But, of course, Jax wouldn't let anyone put that kind of nonsense into the universe. He pushed himself so hard in therapy that he far exceeded anything the doctor expected of him. He still had a long road ahead of him, but with the progress he was making, she felt positive about his prognosis.

She stood up and grabbed the walker, leaning against the wall of the house. Setting it in front of him, she warned the dog, "Stay back, boy," as Whiskey jumped around and tried to get under Jax's feet. She placed her hands under his arms, helping to steady him as he stood up from the chair and transferred his weight onto the walker. "Nothing better than feeling like a toddler learning to walk again when you're my age," he said.

"You're thirty, not eighty, Jax," she said, with a playful roll of her eyes.

He pushed the walker forward and took a step. "Tell that to my body."

"Maybe don't aim for the tree next time," she said, winking at him.

He glanced at her with a sarcastic glare. "Oh, you have all the jokes this morning." He winced as he stepped down on his rehabilitating leg, turning his head slightly before taking another step. They took it slowly, walking down the path toward Jax's place on the back of the property. Whiskey ran up ahead of them, skipping through the tall grass beyond the trees. "I know I told you I was up on Church Run to see Mom."

She bit her lip and grimaced. "Don't tell me there was some other reason."

"No, I went up there to see Mom, and I should have been paying more attention. The whole thing was my own damn fault. I was so distracted and angry." He shook his head. "Obviously, I didn't want to tell you the entire story."

"I assumed not. I know you loved Mom, but graveyards aren't exactly your go-to place." He slowed his steps before looking around the property. She knew she needed to be patient, to let him tell her the story he had been waiting to reveal.

"Mom loved it here," he whispered, his voice hoarse. "She, uh, she and Dad built my house out back, you know?"

She shook her head, remembering her dad telling her the story after she had gotten older how they had built the cabin on the back of the property as a sort of getaway for them to go to when they wanted to pretend they weren't home. "I remember."

"I found some papers in Dad's desk, from some realtor in Erie, Chip something, I don't remember the asshole's name. Anyway, it was an offer for the shop."

Her eyes widened. "Dad is selling the shop?"

"That's what we fought about the night of my accident," he said, as he pushed the walker forward and resumed his journey toward his cabin. "I went to the bar with the papers in my jacket to show Dylan first, but I didn't know what to tell him. He gets so anxious about everything," he continued. "So, instead, I went to the shop to make Dad explain it to me."

"What did he say?" Her heart pounded, desperately trying to understand the situation.

He chuckled and replied, "He admitted it. He has this idea in his brain that he wants to travel the country. Can you believe that? Dad riding around in an RV like some old fogey."

Suddenly, her conversation with Blake's mom and the reason she felt compelled to share that specific story made more sense. "I don't know what to think, Jax," she confessed.

Concerned, he frowned. "I asked him what he expected Dylan and I to do. He just wants to throw everything away, get rid of the shop like it means nothing, and leave Mom behind like she never mattered."

Her brother's face was stoic and firm, but his eyes filled with so much emotion. "You don't actually believe that Jax. Dad loved Mom so much."

"Then why is he running?" he shouted, turning toward her with anger.

With a sigh, she responded, "I don't think he's running. I think he's finally trying to live." Reaching out, she slid her hand along her brother's as it rested on the walker. "But that doesn't mean he cares about her any less."

"Lancaster's Auto Repair is my life," he said firmly. "It's my history, and it's what I love to do." He ran his hand through his hair. "It's all I've ever done. Why wouldn't he talk to us before he just gave away our legacy?"

"I don't know, Jax," she said. "But have you told him how you feel about the shop, or did you just come at him with accusations and anger?"

"Do you even know me at all?"

She laughed. "That's what I thought." As they reached his cabin door, she paused and looked up at her big brother. "I think we need to have a family meeting with Dad."

He nodded. "Can it wait until after Thanksgiving? I just want to eat and enjoy some football before I have to get into my feelings."

She snorted and opened the door to the cabin. "You're an idiot." However, her annoyance was quickly replaced by a grimace as she entered the room and noticed that she had forgotten to clean up the last time she was here—blankets on the couch and wine glasses on the end table next to the fireplace.

She heard her brother whistle behind her. "You're gonna owe me so much after this," he said with a knowing smirk on his face. "Using my place for your secret sex den while I was laid up in a hospital bed, not knowing if I was ever gonna walk again." Annoyed, she looked at him as he added the last punch. "I didn't know you had it in you, sis."

She knew she would never hear the end of this.

Casey

ok it isnt funny anymore

Casey

you are going to make me do something drastic

Casey

are you ignoring my texts to get a rise out of me?

Casey

there are better ways to do that Sammy!

Chapter Eighteen

Blake

Thanksgiving turned out to be one of the best holidays the Lancasters and Forresters had celebrated together in years. With Sam sitting next to him at the dinner table, her hand drifting to his thigh throughout the evening, their fingers intertwining under the table, he couldn't help but smile.

Even Mr. Lancaster and his mom seemed to enjoy reminiscing over stories from the past, embarrassing their children with tales of the five of them until everyone was laughing over shared memories.

Mostly, it was a relaxing time, despite the scowls he continued to receive from his *ex*-best friend on the other side of the table. Though, he put up with Dylan's occasional disparaging remarks, as long as it meant he could steal a small kiss from Sam in the kitchen while everyone else was occupied.

The days after the holiday were spent cozied up on the couch, watching television after work, or hanging out at the Lancaster house. Jax would grumble about the state of his recovery while playing with Whiskey in the backyard, getting better with each passing day.

Blake almost hated how quickly Jax appeared to be recovering, because it meant that Sam would return to Pittsburgh soon.

He wasn't ready to lose her yet.

Sitting at the diner on a cold December evening, with his arm wrapped around Sam's back as they sat across from Jax, felt odd. He wasn't used to being a patron in his own place. Jax was still chewing through his last bite of hamburger as Sam energetically laughed at whatever he said, and Blake simply watched her.

Blake tried to tune into the conversation, glancing over at Sam, mesmerized by her smile. He didn't know how he had never noticed how beautiful she was before she returned to town.

As he stared at her, lost in his thoughts, Sam caught him. "What's wrong?"

He shook his head, absentmindedly twirling a strand of her curly locks around his fingers. "Nothing, you're just really pretty."

Interrupting their moment, Jax sarcastically growled, "Could you two wait until I finish my food before you make me vomit?" He tossed his napkin to his plate, clearly unimpressed.

Just then, the door to the diner opened, the soft jingle alerting them to new guests. A tall man with blond hair entered, looking like one of those guys who appeared to work out but probably never had to a day in his life. He seemed familiar, but Blake couldn't place where he had seen him before.

Returning his focus to the conversation at the table, Blake smiled absentmindedly as Jax started talking about his plans to fix up a new bike after Christmas. However, when he looked up again, he noticed the tall blond man walking toward them, his eyes fixed on Sam. Instinctively, Blake's arm tightened around her shoulder protectively. He couldn't understand why the man continued to approach, his narrowed eyes searching for recognition as he got closer to their table. He glanced away, perhaps hoping that maybe the guy would just go away if he stopped looking at him.

Suddenly, the man was standing directly in front of their table. "There's my girl."

Everyone at the table looked up, startled by his presence. Blake turned to Sam, who was staring back at the man in shock. "Casey, what are you doing here?" she asked, the surprise clear on her face.

"You've been ignoring my texts, baby girl," he said, dropping his backpack onto the floor at Blake's feet and holding his arms out wide, "so, here I am."

Baby girl? Sam was ignoring his texts?

Blake turned to look at Sam, a questioning look in his eye. "Sam?"

"Oh, um—Blake, this is Casey. Casey, Blake." Then Sam turned to her brother. "And this is my brother, Jax."

Jax sounded annoyed. "You're that guy? This is the wanker that Dylan always complains about?"

Blake couldn't help but laugh, but Sam discreetly pressed her leg against his under the table. "Jax!" she scolded.

Casey seemed proud. "I see my reputation precedes me." Blake couldn't help but wonder if Casey was just an idiot.

"I didn't need you to come here, Casey," Sam said anxiously. "I wasn't responding because I was busy."

Casey glanced at Blake, noticing his arm around Sam's shoulder. "I can see that," he said.

Casey grabbed a chair from one of the empty tables and dragged it over, straddling the chair backward as he sat down next to Blake. "So, Blaine—"

"Blake," he quickly reminded him.

Casey ignored the correction. "How do you know our Sammy?" He grinned and winked obnoxiously at Sam, who was growing restless.

It was clear to Blake that Casey was not only an idiot but also a jerk, which aligned with what Sam had already spoken about him. "We grew up together," Blake said, rubbing Sam's shoulder.

"Adorable," Casey said with an obnoxious chuckle.

Kelley approached the table and its new occupant. "Did you want to order something?"

Casey turned toward his sister, his eyes glancing up and down her body in a move that had Blake ready to grab the guy by the collar and rip his eyes out. "God, this town is adorable," Casey said, directing his statement toward Kelley. "How old are you, sweetheart?"

Blake tensed, and Sam immediately shifted beside him. Trying to diffuse the situation, Sam intervened. "Casey, this is Kelley, Blake's little sister."

Casey faced Blake with a grin, "Damn, sorry, Billy."

His jaw tensed as he mumbled his actual name under his breath for the second time. "I'm gonna take it that the only thing you are bringing to the table is a heaping pile of toxic masculinity," Kelley said in frustration. She shoved her pen back in her apron and walked away, shrugging with aggravation.

"She seems like a peach," Casey joked.

Sam sighed. "I think Jax and I should get going." As she spoke, her hand patted Blake's thigh. He frowned in response and leaned over to press a kiss to her lips. In that moment, she appeared surprised, and he couldn't help but wonder if it was because Casey was staring at them intently.

He smoothly slid out of the booth and offered his hand to help Sam up. "I'll walk you out."

Interrupting their departure, Casey turned to Sam. "Sam, are you okay if I crash at your place tonight?" Blake's temper rose as Casey spoke. "I can find a place in the morning, but it's late tonight, so I thought you might let me ride your couch. For old time's sake."

Sam tried to ease the situation by rubbing her hands along Blake's arm. "I'm not sure if that's a good idea, Casey."

Unfazed by the tension, Casey raised his arms and smiled widely. "Come on, sweetness, don't leave me without a bed for the night."

Growing more irritated, Blake growled, "Maybe start by dropping the nicknames."

"Hey, Brian, no harm meant by it," Casey said in a friendly tone. "Sammy and I are...friends, right, Sammy?" Casey grinned.

"It's Blake!" he shouted, causing everyone to turn and stare at him. Blake stood frozen, his fists clenched at his side, trying to control his emotions.

"One night," Sam said, sighing, leaving Blake slightly annoyed and disappointed. She had previously mentioned that she wasn't interested in Casey, yet he was someone she had a connection with back in Pittsburgh and who was now getting to go home with her.

Her hand fell away from his as she walked out of the diner toward her car. He followed her begrudgingly, watching the situation play out in front of him. Annoyingly, Casey got into the back of her car, a shit-eating grin on his face. Sam leaned up on her toes and kissed Blake softly on the lips. "Sorry for today, I'll talk to you tomorrow, alright?" He nodded, reluctantly letting her hand slip from his, watching her walk to the other side of the car.

Jax grumbled, patting Blake on the shoulder. "You want me to stick my walker up his ass?" he said. "Cause you know I'll do it."

"Tempting, but I don't think we should piss off the Pirates' one million Facebook fans," Blake said with a laugh.

"It's your call, boss," Jax said, letting his lips turn up with a grin. "But let me know if you change your mind."

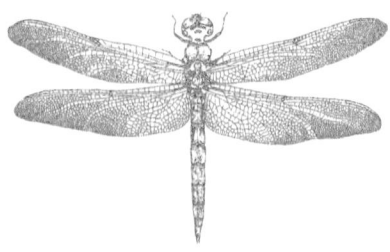

Chapter Nineteen

Samantha

Samantha was annoyed when she got home. She could hardly believe that Casey had come all the way to her hometown to find her just because she ignored his stupid text messages. It made no sense to her. She and Casey didn't have this type of relationship.

She handed him a folded blanket and pillow as he stood in the middle of her living room. "You really are an idiot."

"What, you aren't impressed by my gesture?" He grinned. "Don't tell me you're really interested in that Brian guy."

"His name is Blake, and he's none of your business." She shook her head. "Besides, what are you doing chasing me down here? That's not even your style."

He shrugged. "I'm not allowed to miss you?"

"The only thing you would ever miss is your dick," she said. He returned her remark with a loud, mocking sound.

"Sammy, you make me sound so shallow." He flopped down on the couch, arms spread out, and crossed his legs. "We have fun, don't we? I thought our arrangement was beneficial for both of us."

She shook her head and leaned against her dad's Lazy Boy chair. "Casey, you know I've enjoyed the time we've spent together, but you don't need me. We both know you can have any girl you want, so I'll ask you again, why are you here?"

"I don't know, I like you, and then you weren't there...and..." He paused. "I didn't love that."

She laughed. "Oh please, Casey. That's not it at all. The only thing you don't love is that I'm taking the walk on this."

"Baby, the only balls I've ever thrown your way are between my legs," he said with a smirk.

"Just go home, Casey," she said, pushing away from the couch. Just then, the front door opened. Dylan walked in and looked at her, clearly surprised to see her home.

However, nothing compared to the shock he found when his eyes fell on Casey. "What the hell is he doing here?" he said.

"If it isn't my favorite pen-pal," Casey said sarcastically.

"Casey will be gone tomorrow," she said emphatically.

"Yeah, whatever," Dylan said with a loud groan. "The sooner the better." He strode through the room, then climbed the stairs two at a time toward his room.

"So, where does a guy go around here for a little fun?" The grin on his face told her he wasn't thinking about leaving first thing in the morning.

"It's a small town, remember? You hate those, so just go home, please," she pleaded. "I'm going to bed." She walked toward the stairs, shutting off the lights behind her.

"You want company, Sammy?" his voice sang from the darkness.

She climbed the stairs, ignoring his request. "Goodnight, Casey."

She woke to the sound of her phone vibrating on the nightstand the next morning. The smile on her face grew as she read Blake's messages.

Blake

morning, beautiful

Blake

hope you had a beautiful stress-free morning

Blake

Boondocks after my shift tonight?

She laughed at his passive aggressive message, sure that the stress he was referencing was none other than Casey Anderson.

I have some stuff to do with Jax today but Boondocks sounds perfect!

Look forward to seeing you Xx

She ignored the flip-flop her stomach did reading his text; two little x's meant nothing. After all, she wasn't in high school anymore. She had outgrown the days of writing boy's names in her notepads with hearts and glitter. Sam wasn't prone to giddy daydreaming or scrawling her name alongside a boy's last name. She was practical. It was what she had to be.

Expecting to find Casey still on the sofa, she skipped down the stairs. However, to her surprise, she discovered the pillow and blankets neatly folded on the edge of the couch. Her father's voice drifted in through the open front door, where he sat on the porch with his morning coffee. "He left this morning."

Feeling a sense of relief, she exhaled. Casey had taken her words to heart and had gone back to Pittsburgh. She poured herself a cup of coffee and joined her dad on the porch. As she took a seat beside him on the swing that had been hung when she was six, her dad laughed. "Never a dull moment with you around, Dragonfly."

Sipping her coffee, she tucked her legs up under her chin and pulled the blanket around her body, snuggling in. "Sorry for all that last night. I'm sure you weren't expecting company."

"It's not often the star pitcher of the Pittsburgh Pirates shows up at your front door asking to 'ride your couch' for the night," he said with a smirk, glancing at her.

Still annoyed that it had even happened, she shook her head and moaned. "Yeah, well, that's Casey for you."

"I thought it wasn't serious between the two of you?" His gravelly voice was calm and full of concern.

"It was never serious. Casey—well, he enjoys being the center of attention. I guess I've been busy with other things, and he suddenly felt ignored, so he came looking for his attention instead," she explained with a grunt.

Her dad nodded, showing some understanding. "And these other things you were busy with, would they just be helping your brother, or would that include our Forrester fellow?"

"Daddy!" she said with a shocked wail before biting her lip. "You know, Jax has kept me plenty busy."

"And I know you spent a lot of time with that boy in your brother's cabin before Jax got out of the hospital," he said, turning to her to wave off her wide eyes. "Oh, don't give me that look. You may be the baby, but that doesn't mean you are any better at hiding things from your dear old dad than your brothers are."

"Why didn't you say anything?" she asked softly, prompting him to chuckle and sip his coffee.

"Blake's good for you," he said, taking a moment to pause. "He's a good kid."

"Daddy, I don't live here. It's never going to work with us," she said, her voice tinged with sadness. "Blake will never leave his mom or the diner."

"Dragonfly, there is one thing I learned when I realized your mom was the one for me," he began, his gaze drifting off into the distance. "Love changes a man, it rearranges who you are. When you love someone else, you'll do anything for them."

"Like staying in Titusville for Mom?" she asked, watching his eyes glance down toward his hands, his fingers absentmindedly fiddling with the gold band still on his finger.

"Titusville has always been home," he said, his voice filled with a mix of longing and determination.

"Mom would want you to be happy, even now." She hesitated, not wanting to push him further, sensing his walls closing up.

"I'm happy, Dragonfly. I've got my kids, and..." he trailed off, his eyes distant.

"Dad, I know about Erie," she said, causing his hand to still in his lap, the coffee cup trembling slightly. "I know about the offer and the night of Jax's accident. What I don't understand is why you didn't talk to any of us about it."

He sighed regretfully. "I didn't want you kids to be disappointed in me."

"Why would we ever be disappointed in you?" she asked, shocked by his admission.

"I know I wasn't the best parent after your mom died," he confessed, his voice wavering. "I did the best I could with you kids, but your mom was the one who had all the answers. Hell, I raised you like your brothers. There are so many things I did wrong."

Her hand reached out to grasp his, offering comfort. "I can't speak for my brothers, but I never could have asked for a better dad. You did the best you could with the three of us. We didn't make it easy for you either. You raised three stubborn ass kids," she said, chuckling lightly. "You weren't perfect, but you were ours."

"I think it might be time for me to do something for me for once," he murmured. "And that feels mighty selfish."

"Daddy, we're adults. We can all take care of ourselves, despite evidence to the contrary lately," she said with a laugh. "And maybe there are other options besides Erie that you haven't thought of."

He turned toward her with a look of surprise. "And what options might those be, exactly?"

"Maybe you should think about calling a Lancaster family meeting soon." She quirked her eyebrow and smiled.

Chapter Twenty

Blake

B lake regretted coming to Boondocks early. He should have just waited for Sam to text him, telling him she was on her way. However, he figured it couldn't hurt to head in and get a head start on a beer. Unfortunately for him, two things stood in his way of a nice relaxing beer.

Casey Anderson and Dylan Lancaster were both sitting at the bar.

Dylan appeared to be sulking at one end of the bar, his shoulders slouching over a glass of something clear (it sure as hell wasn't water). Casey, on the other hand, was positioned a few seats down from him, nursing a Bud Light. So not only was the guy an idiot, a jackass, and a complete moron, he also had really shit taste in beer.

Blake made his way to the opposite end of the bar, purposely avoiding Dylan. Rusty acknowledged him as the stool scraped along the wooden floor. "What can I get you, Blake?" Rusty asked.

"Whiskey sour," Blake said, amending his need for a simple beer after assessing the stress of the situation he found himself in.

Dylan looked up from his glass and glared in his direction, tossing back whatever was in there. "Another," he said, slamming his glass back on the counter.

"Can you believe the way that guy rushed the passer?" Casey's voice lifted over the noise of the Big and Rich song that started playing over the jukebox. He paused, chewing on a wad of chewing gum. "This is my song," he hollered with a loud whoop. "Save a horse, ride a cowboy." His annoying voice got louder as he started to sing.

Dylan, clearly annoyed, growled without looking up from his newly poured drink. "Shut the hell up," he grumbled as he put the glass to his mouth and then swallowed with a gulp, tossing his head back.

"You got a real problem with me, but it ain't my fault your sister enjoyed the ride." Casey winked at Dylan, causing Blake to flinch at the insult.

In response, Dylan slammed his glass on the bar and lifted the brim of his Steelers cap off his forehead. "The hell you just say about my sister?"

Recognizing that the situation was escalating, Blake stepped in and tried to defuse the tension. "Hey, why don't you just drink that piss you call beer and get the hell out of town like Sam asked?"

"Don't get involved in this," Dylan said, shooting him a menacing glance.

Casey giggled. "Looks like you and me got something in common, Ole Billy boy. Dylan don't like us."

Blake, not wanting to be associated with Casey, spat back, "You and I have nothing in common, asshole."

"Besides fucking my sister," Dylan grumbled.

"At least he didn't have sex with my girlfriend," Blake shot back angrily.

"Whoo-wee." Casey whistled. "Seems you two have some issues to work out."

"Go to hell," Dylan spat at the ballplayer, hanging his head as he rested them on his palms.

Amidst the escalating tension, Casey stood up from the bar, dancing to 'his song' while pointing at Dylan. "Did you know that your sister and I used to stay up all night making love to this song?"

Blake was ready to take matters into his own hands and punch Casey in the mouth, but before he could get off his stool, Dylan was already in Casey's face, his hand on his chest, forcefully shoving him back toward his stool.

Trying to assert authority, Dylan's voice was loud and assertive. "My sister asked you to leave."

However, Casey, who was over six feet tall and towered over Dylan's 5'10 frame, taunted, "Woah little man, might want to step back there, Dilly."

Dylan was never one to back down from a fight, regardless of who had the advantage, and Blake recognized the moment the switch was flipped in Dylan's demeanor. His eyes grew darker, a smirk played on his face, and almost perfectly synchronized with the chorus, his fist connected with Casey's cheek.

In that split second, everything unfolded simultaneously.

Casey swiftly recovered, his fist coming up from behind as it caught Dylan in the ear. He watched Casey push Dylan backward, pinning him against the wall with repeated blows to his gut.

Sensing the urgency, Blake rushed forward and grabbed Casey by the shoulder, swiftly swinging him away from Dylan. Blake puffed out his chest, stood tall, and lifted his chin to meet Casey's gaze. "Why don't you pick on someone your own size?" he said, issuing a challenge, his fists clenched.

"You want some of this, Bobby?" Casey gestured for Blake to come closer.

Blake responded by raising his fists. "My father was Bobby, asshole. I'm Blake," he said, striking Casey squarely in the jaw. Blake relished the way Casey's head jerked backward before quickly regaining composure and wiping the blood from his fingers after touching his chin.

Casey licked his lips and smirked. "Okay, Blake—"

Before he could finish his sentence, Blake interrupted him with another punch. Casey stumbled for a moment but retaliated by lunging at Blake with full force, knocking the wind out of him and sending them both tumbling to the ground. The ringing in Blake's ears from the powerful blow to the side of his head momentarily disoriented him.

Then, to his surprise, Casey was on the ground beside him, and Dylan loomed over them, delivering a punch to Casey's face. In a desperate move, Casey kicked Dylan's leg, causing him to stumble toward the ground.

Blake took advantage of the moment of confusion to roll over onto his stomach and swiftly climb to his feet. However, before he could regain his bearings, a pair of arms wrapped around his waist, propelling him forcefully backward onto the table. The table couldn't withstand their combined weight, causing it to break, and they both went crashing to the ground.

The impact was followed by a blow to his chest, causing him to gasp for air and clutch his chest in pain. In a swift response, Dylan intervened and pulled Casey away from Blake. As Blake struggled to catch his breath and regain his balance, a commotion erupted on the other side of the bar, abruptly silencing the music.

A commanding voice put an end to the chaos. "Enough!" Blake was then grabbed by another pair of arms, forcefully restraining him as his hands were violently pulled behind his back and he felt a cold metal clasp around each wrist. The imposing figure of Sheriff Draper emerged from the doorway, blocking the light, as he came into view. His burly face was hard-set as he commanded, "Take em' to the sheriff's office." He paused. "Make sure to read 'em their rights."

Well, hell!

As Blake shook his head to clear the dirt and debris from his hair, he glanced up and saw Sam's horrified gaze fixed upon him. It was unclear when she had arrived or how much of the fight she had witnessed, but the look on her face conveyed that she had seen enough.

Sitting in the small cell, Blake rested his head against the hard concrete wall and closed his eyes. Not in all of his twenty-eight years of life had he ever been arrested before. Though he had been in fights in town, it had never led to an arrest. He was sure his mother was going to be pissed. Not to mention the fact that the look of disappointment on Sam's face weighed heavily on his mind. In frustration, he lifted his head and lightly smacked it against the wall, exhaling deeply.

Across the cell, Dylan sat on the ground, his gaze fixed on the offices beyond where they were being held. "You didn't have to get involved, you know," Dylan said quietly.

Blake simply shrugged and replied, "Always back up your best friend."

Their eyes met. "Even after everything?" he asked skeptically.

Blake's response was clear and unwavering. "Especially after everything," he said firmly. His gaze shifted toward the next cell, where Casey was sulking, lying on a cot with his back turned to them.

Dylan's grumbling interrupted the silence. "It's not your job to protect her, you know."

Blake let out a heavy breath, contemplating his own feelings. "What if I want it to be?" he finally voiced.

The tension in the air escalated as Casey's voice carried across the cell. Dylan and Blake turned toward him, seeing him sitting up on his cot, staring at them. "You're both dumbasses!" he said. "Do either of you realize that Sam Lancaster is one of the baddest bitches I've ever met? She doesn't actually need anyone to protect her."

Dylan, defensive of his sister, argued back, "You know nothing about my sister."

Casey shook his head, responding with a hint of frustration. "I know she doesn't need you texting any man she looks at, warning them to leave her alone."

Dylan interjected, "I only did that with you because you fuck anything that moves, and she deserves better than that."

"Maybe you have a point there, but what's your excuse with him?" Casey asked, pointing at Blake. "Seems like he actually cares about her." Dylan glanced at Blake and frowned. "But maybe you'd realize that if you weren't screwing around behind his back. Is it guilt that makes you an asshole, or?"

"She's my little sister. No one's good enough." He shook his head and shrugged. "Though I guess if I was gonna pick anyone for Sam, Blake's a pretty good guy and maybe the only guy good enough for her."

Warmth spread in Blake's chest, a smile forming on his lips. "I just want her to be happy." Blake realized that was all he really cared about for Sam—her happiness.

"See, that's the difference between you and me," Casey said slowly. "I came here because I missed her." Blake scrunched his forehead in confusion. Wasn't missing her a sign of strong feelings for someone? "But I didn't miss her because I love her. I missed her because of what she provides for me. Attention, that's all." He laughed with a smirk. "The only person I'm capable of loving is myself. Sam knows this, I know this. For a while, that worked for us."

Dylan shook his head against the bars. "You're an egotistical freak, you know that?"

"Yeah, but I'm damn good at it," he said with a laugh. "Anyway, Sam seemed fine with our little situation before she came back here. I'm guessing whatever reason that's changed has to do with you."

Blake wanted to believe that was true. He wanted to hope that Sam cared about him, that she could possibly love him. However, a part of him wondered if it would even matter. If he told her how he felt about her, if he expressed his feelings, told her he loved her, then what? Would she want a long-distance relationship with him? And did he even want that?

Just as he was lost in these thoughts, the deputy walked into the room, interrupting them. "Casey Anderson?" the deputy called out.

"That's me," Casey said, standing up from his cot.

"Your agent is here to bail you out," the deputy announced, and Casey smiled at them.

"Well, boys, it was fun, but it looks like our time here has come to an end. Can's say it was nice meeting you, but it was the most fun I've had in a while." Casey glanced at Dylan and added, "And lose my number, will ya?"

Dylan sighed and sunk against the bars, waving his middle finger as the baseball player was released from his cell. Casey glanced at Blake as he was being led out. "You treat her good, you hear, Blake?"

Blake nodded and watched Casey leave the office. He let his head rest against the concrete wall again as his eyes fell shut once more.

When the silence settled over them again, Dylan spoke. "I'm sorry about Donna. I know I fucked up and I have no excuse," he said as he opened his eyes to see Dylan staring at him. "My guilt has been eating me alive."

Blake shrugged. "I'm sorry I didn't tell you about Sam."

Dylan scrunched his nose and frowned. "Yeah, well, walking in on *that* is not something I ever care to see again! I'm still having nightmares."

"Grow up," Blake said, though thoughts of his own sister and another person brought about the same sense of dread as Dylan experienced, and he felt some sympathy for his friend. "I care about Sam," he said.

"You damn well better be in love with her after what I witnessed, or I swear to God." Dylan's face was serious, but a smile grew on his lips. "I don't want to have to give you the intentions speech, but seriously, what are your intentions with my sister, dude?"

"I've been trying to put it into words for weeks," he said, groaning.

Dylan chuckled. "I knew you got hit a lot in football, but it's three words dude, *I love you!* Seriously, it's not that hard."

"What if she doesn't feel the same way?" Blake's head rested against the concrete wall. "Pittsburgh isn't Titusville. She works with baseball players who make millions of dollars all day long."

"You mean like that asshat we just beat up? Yeah, he's a real winner. I'm sure she'd pick him every day over my best friend." Dylan smiled sincerely.

For the first time in weeks, Blake felt like things might be alright between him and Dylan. "You mean that?" he asked.

"Hell no, she's not going to choose him." Dylan's forehead pinched in confusion.

"No." He laughed. "I mean, are you really still my best friend?"

"Always, man, ride or die. Nothing is ever going to change that," Dylan said with a nod.

"What do I do about Sam?" Blake asked with a sigh.

"Good luck with that, buddy. We never figured out how to read a chick's mind, definitely never have with my sister. So, the only way you're gonna know how she feels about you is if you man up and tell her how you feel about her," Dylan said with a chuckle.

Blake groaned and closed his eyes once more, trying to figure out how he was going to tell Sam Lancaster that he was in love with her.

Chapter Twenty-One

Samantha

A light dusting of snow covered the ground, while snowflakes continued to drift slowly onto the lawn. Sam sat on the swing, wrapped in a blanket and holding a cup of hot chocolate. As she enjoyed the peaceful scene, her iPod played a Sabrina Carpenter tune, and she hummed along to the lyrics of "Bad for Business" as thoughts of the fight at the bar that night crossed her mind.

Anger surged within her as she remembered seeing Blake, Casey, and Dylan in the middle of the floor, throwing punches and kicking each other like children fighting over a toy. It was frustrating to witness such ridiculous behavior.

Just then, a sports car pulled into her driveway, interrupting her thoughts. Sam removed her headphones, replacing the music with the sound of thumping from the car's radio.

Casey turned off the engine and stepped out of the car, his eyes fixed on her from the driver's side door. Frowning, she slumped her shoulders as he cautiously approached her. "Hey, Sammy," he greeted.

"Don't you Sammy me!" she lectured, her tone filled with frustration. "I told you to go home, and instead I find you in a brawl with my brother and my..." she paused, realizing she had no idea how she was about to identify Blake.

"I know, I'm sorry," Casey said, surprisingly sincere. "I should have listened to you, but I was having fun. What can I say?"

"Which part of screwing up my life was fun?" she said, raising her voice, crossing her arms.

He nodded, acknowledging his mistake. "You're right."

"Why didn't you just go home like I asked you to?" Sam's voice trembled with vulnerability and anxiety.

"You know why," he said, shrugging. "You ignored me. I hate that. I just wanted to get your attention again. I thought there was no way you were really interested in this small-town loser. I mean, come on Sammy, he's just a cook. What's could he possibly have that I don't?"

"Casey!" she said, her tone firm. "Blake is more than just a cook. He's supportive, loyal, and an amazing friend."

"Friend..." Casey let the word hang in the air for a moment. "It seems like he might be more than that," he said, his eyebrow lifting playfully. "It's not like you to catch feelings, Sammy."

"Okay, that's enough, Casanova," she said, shaking her head with a laugh. She used the nickname all the girls at work had given him because of his history with women, knowing it drove home her point. "You and I don't have the kind of relationship where we gossip like girlfriends."

"We could, you know," he said with a boyish and charming grin. "You and I could keep things light, snuggle up with a bottle of wine and...But you're not looking for that anymore, are you?"

Her sigh was longing and soft. "I thought that was all I needed, that I could live with that," she said, as she patted his hand. "But I want more, and you can't give me that."

Casey chimed in with a friendly wink, pointing to the bruise on his chin. "Maybe you should talk to the guy who can," he said. "This wasn't no friends-with-benefits love chat."

She shook her head and chuckled. "Go home, Casey."

Hours later, Dylan and her father arrived home. Jax and Sam had been patiently waiting on the couch for their arrival. As soon as Dylan approached Sam, she stood up and wrapped her arms around his neck. "You are an idiot," she said, in a tone that was both firm but full of affection.

Dylan's laughter reverberated against her neck as he pulled her closer, his arms encircling her waist. "I'm so sorry, Sam," he said sincerely.

Pulling back slightly, Dylan locked eyes with her. "What were you thinking, going after a baseball player, Dylan?" she asked, full of concern.

"That guy is an asshole, and he said some really offensive things," he said, defending himself, but then paused. "But you're right, it was stupid to start an argument with him."

"Dylan, I can protect myself. I don't need you fighting my battles for me," Sam said in protest.

Taking a seat on the couch, Dylan sighed, and Sam settled in beside him. "Ever since you moved away, I just feel like...like you're out there on your own, and I'm helpless to do anything," he confessed.

Jax, hobbling over to a seat across from the couch, chimed in. "I think what our little brother is trying to say in his dumbass way is that he misses you, and he just wants to make sure you're leading a pleasant life. Unfortunately, he goes about it in the most...uh, jackass way."

Dylan groaned. "So eloquently put," he said sarcastically. "But not exactly wrong, either."

Sam tried not to be too harsh on her brother, as she appreciated his concern. He was just looking out for her. "I love you, Dilly Bear," she said, brushing her hand through his hair. "But you gotta let me grow up."

Dylan frowned and held her hand. "Maybe I'm just not ready to let you go."

Sam shook her head. "Like you could ever get rid of me," she said, "you wouldn't know what to do without texting me every morning."

Jax, overhearing this comment, groaned and shook his head. "You text her every morning? Jesus! The hell is the matter with you?"

"It's not my fault I'm her favorite and you are just the second brother," Dylan said, preening.

Jax scoffed. "You punched her boyfriend in the face. I'm pretty sure you lost some status there."

Dylan turned toward Sam, narrowing his eyes. "Wait, wait, boyfriend? No one told me Blake graduated to the boyfriend rank." He playfully tickled her side.

Sam giggled and pushed his hands away, blushing. "No one is using the B word."

"And why not? Is my best friend not good enough for you?" Dylan asked sarcastically.

Her lips parted in confusion. "Wait, now you want me to date Blake?"

"He's a good guy. You won't find anyone better. Obviously, you find him attractive. God forbid I'll never be able to bleach my eyes from the way I found you two." Shaking his head and closing his eyes as if wiping his memory, he responded, "So what's the problem, and please tell me it's not because of that asshole, Casey?"

"Good Lord, no, Casey and I, it was never serious." She let out a loud sigh. "But Blake, well, I live in Pittsburgh, and he doesn't."

Dylan scoffed. "Have you never heard of a cell phone?"

Jax even chimed in, laughing, "Phone sex, dick pics, sexy texts, come on, sis, these are all things in the 2020s."

Sam groaned. "Can you two not? I'm just not sure we can make it work."

Dylan turned toward her. "Do you love him or not?"

Sam twisted the necklace on her neck, biting her lip. After a moment, she hesitantly answered, "I—I think that it's not that simple."

"Oh, bullshit sis. You've liked this guy since you were a teenager," Jax said.

Surprised, Dylan exclaimed, wide-eyed, "What? You liked Blake when we were kids?"

Feeling uncomfortable, she shifted on the couch anxiously. "Can you not be weird about this?"

Dylan seemed to be deciding how he wanted to reply. "So, if you've liked him all this time, just tell him."

"He knows I've liked him for a while, but love is a whole unfamiliar territory for us, me especially, and I'm not sure if he's in the same place as me," she admitted.

Dylan smiled, playfully pushing her shoulder. "Only one way to find out, sis."

Jax simply shrugged, and Sam considered that maybe her brothers were both right for the first time in her entire life.

Chapter Twenty-Two

Blake

B lake sat at the desk, watching as his mother signed some papers at Officer Humble's desk. Fidgeting with his fingers and biting his lip, he grew increasingly impatient with the time it was taking. His friend Dylan had already left with his dad twenty minutes ago, making Blake wonder why this process was dragging on. Suddenly, Sheriff Draper entered the room, slamming a folder on the desk next to Blake. "Always getting into trouble, aren't you, Blake?" he said with a sneer.

Startled, Blake flinched but defiantly met the sheriff's gaze. "I didn't start the fight," he said.

"That's always your excuse, isn't it?" the sheriff said gruffly. "Nothing but trouble."

Sensing tension, Blake's mother quickly approached. "Is there a problem here?" she asked, raising her voice. "Because the charges were dropped, Sheriff."

Blake was surprised to hear about the dropped charges, as no one had informed him or provided an explanation. Sheriff Draper dismissively responded, "Technicality. Just because Mr. Anderson used his clout to get these charges dropped doesn't mean that Blake isn't a—"

Blake's mother intervened in a stern and forceful tone. "If you say one more word about my son, Albert, I'm going to file a complaint with the department."

The man studied his mother and seemed to be thinking through her words before he grunted and nodded at her. "Fine, Linda, you're free to go." Her firmness seemed to weaken the sheriff momentarily, as he begrudgingly waved his hand and exited the room with a grunt.

His mother touched his shoulder, looking at him reassuringly with a smile. "Let's go home, sweetie."

Blake sadly nodded and followed her out the door. "I'm sorry about this, Mom. I know it was stupid."

"Oh, honey, you and Dylan have been doing stupid things together since you were four years old. The fact that you are in love with Samantha only adds a new layer to the level at which your stupidity will take you," she said with a laugh.

"Gee, thanks, Mom," he said with a groan, not even bothering to deny her statement.

"Ignore Albert Draper. That man was a bore, even back in high school. He hated your father for beating him out as head quarterback and he's never gotten over it. Now, let's get you home and get you cleaned up." Patting his hand, she smiled. "I think you have some things you should talk about with Samantha."

Chuckling, Blake nodded. "Thanks, Mom. I think you might be right."

"How'd it feel to get arrested?" Kelley teased when he arrived home.

Blake, crossing his arms over his chest, winced at the pain coursing through his body. He was hurting all over and all he wanted was to take a shower. "Honestly, it felt like shit," he said.

"Maybe don't act like shit then," she deadpanned with a glare.

"Thanks for your advice, Kels. It was oh-so-helpful," he said sarcastically, just as the doorbell rang. The last thing he wanted was someone else to talk to.

With frustration, he yanked the door open. "What?"

On the other side of the door stood Donna Draper, dressed scantly—considering the weather—in a miniskirt and crop top. "Oh my God, Blake!" she said with a squeal, seemingly oblivious to his bad mood. "I just heard that you got released, and I had to come see you right away to make sure you were alright."

"Donna, I'm really not in the mood for this today," he said, sighing.

"Can I come in? I just wanted to apologize," she said morosely, shifting on her feet.

He closed his eyes and frowned. "Apologize for what?"

"Your arrest was my fault."

Suddenly, Donna burst into tears, leaving Blake unsure how to react. He opened the door further, and she rushed into the house.

Kelley watched the display and looked between them, disgusted. "I'm going to my room." She groaned, then disappeared down the hallway, leaving Blake alone with an overreacting Donna.

When they were alone, he turned to Donna. "So, how is this your fault?"

Through her sobs, she explained, "I was just so jealous of you and Sam. And then that Casey guy showed up, and it felt unfair that she had both of you there, fighting over her." Blake rolled his eyes at her theatrics, but she continued sobbing. "So, I called my dad when the fighting broke out."

He sighed, wishing she would just leave, but he honestly just wanted her to calm down. "Alright, look, it's fine."

Wiping her eyes, she looked up at him. "But I got you arrested."

Knowing the only way to get her to leave was to get her to realize he wasn't upset with her, he quickly reassured her, "The charges got dropped, so everything turned out fine."

Sniffling softly, she looked up at him with big blue eyes, her red lips in a pout. This used to work on him in the past, this game she always played, the manipulation she was so good at. As expected, she lunged for him, wrapping her arms around his neck. "So, you forgive me?"

He reached back, grabbing her hands and prying them away from his neck. Stepping away from her, he tried to make himself clear to her. "Donna, I need you to understand that this is never going to happen between us again."

She whimpered. "But you just said you forgive me?"

Pushing her hands away, Blake responded firmly, "Look, you and me, we just don't work."

She spat, "Is this because of her? Because of Sam? What does she have that I don't?"

Rubbing the bruise on his face, he shook his head. "It's not about Sam, not entirely. It's about us, and I just don't love you," he groaned in frustration.

Her next words were shot venomously at him. "But you love *her*?"

With a soft smile, he replied with the honest truth. "I do." Gripping his side, he walked past her, wanting nothing more than a shower and peace and quiet. "I believe you know where the door is, Donna. Goodbye."

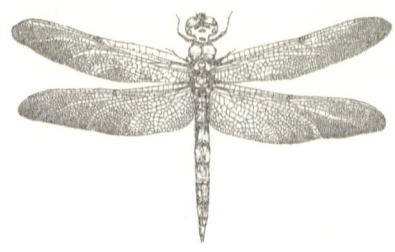

Chapter Twenty-Three

Samantha

S am stood in front of Blake's door; her mind filled with uncertainty. Was she really about to tell him she was in love with him? Doubt crept in as she turned around to leave, finding herself standing in the middle of the walkway, engaged in a heated conversation with herself. It was as if she had lost control, talking to herself like a crazy person.

But deep down, she couldn't deny her feelings for Blake. She believed he deserved to know the truth. It was an opportunity for both of them to find happiness, and she owed it to herself to find out if he felt the same way.

With determination in her eyes, she turned back toward the door. Step by step, she walked firmly up to it, raising her hand to knock just as the front door swung open unexpectedly. The sight of Donna Draper greeting her caught her off guard.

"Sam Lancaster, to what do we owe the pleasure of your visit after all the trouble you've caused?" Donna's words stung, causing

Sam to flinch momentarily. However, she quickly regained her composure, her focus solely on finding Blake.

Ignoring Donna's presence, Sam asked the woman, "Where's Blake? I'm not in the mood to talk to you right now." Donna giggled—an unsettling sound that made Sam even more determined to see Blake.

"He's upstairs, pretty banged up after the fight," Donna said, amused by the situation. Sam's confusion grew. Why was Donna here? And why was she answering the door for the Forresters?

"Can you just let me in so I can talk to Blake?" Sam said, with agitation.

"He doesn't want to talk to you right now." Sam's surprise was evident, but Donna seemed to revel in it, her blonde hair framing a smirk on her face.

"I'm sorry, what?" Sam said, her voice betraying her shock.

Donna continued, seemingly unfazed by Sam's reaction. "Yeah, after the fight, Blake and I had a long talk. He feels like you're not a good influence on his life." Sam couldn't believe what she was hearing. She snorted in disbelief, but Donna carried on, disregarding her outburst. "The fight opened his eyes to what truly matters to him. He and I are giving our relationship another chance."

Sam's throat tightened, her heart sinking as she struggled to process the news. "Oh," was all she said, her voice strained with emotion. Donna's next words hit her like a punch to the gut.

"Yeah, you know how important his hometown is to him. With you going back to Pittsburgh soon, he didn't see a future with someone who doesn't share his priorities."

Sam swallowed hard, blinking away the tears threatening to spill. Nausea churned in her stomach as she realized that her chance at happiness with Blake was slipping away.

Sam Lancaster would not cry!

Sam sat on her bed, staring at the wall. Maybe this was for the best. Perhaps she should never have dared to dream about having a future with Blake. It was a daydream, and Sam didn't daydream.

She closed her eyes, cursing the hope she had given herself. Angry that she even dared to listen to her brothers, to Casey, even her father. She should have stayed true to herself, stayed within the walls of her heart and now...she had allowed her walls to drop. It was a mistake.

She couldn't afford to make mistakes. Her cheeks felt wet, and she reached up and wiped at the moisture. Anger overwhelmed her as she felt the first tears fall. She pressed her palms to her eyes, willing the tears to stop. *Do not cry!*

She growled angrily, standing up from her bed and pacing the floor anxiously. This was not an emotion she allowed herself to feel, this deep sadness that threatened to swallow her whole. However, the more she tried to stop the tears, the more they swelled in her eyes. She needed it to stop; she needed to breathe, needed her heart to stop aching. Whatever this emotion was that she was feeling, she wanted it to go away.

Looking around her room, her eyes landing on the photo of her, Dylan and Blake on her desk, it felt as if all the wind was knocked out of her chest, and she felt the need to run. She needed to escape.

She reached under her bed, grabbing her suitcase and pulling it onto her mattress, gathering clothes from her dressers and tossing them into her bag. She had stayed long enough. Perhaps it was time to return to Pittsburgh.

Sam

Lancaster family meeting tomorrow morning.

Sam

got some things I think we all need to discuss!

Quietly, she approached the bench under the old tree. She reached down to brush the light dusting of snow off the concrete before sitting down on the cool surface. As the breeze blew through her hair, making it even messier than usual, she tucked it into her scarf. Looking at the stone in front of her, she smiled softly. "Hey, Mom. Long time no talk."

Tucking her gloved hands under her legs for warmth, she chewed on the inside of her bottom lip. "I guess I should have come and seen you sooner, but you know how much I hate one-sided conversations," she added, sniffling. "I suppose you heard about Jax's accident. He's walking again, but he's still whining about it," she said with a chuckle, the sound echoing around her. "Dylan and I stopped fighting. Don't tell him, but I don't think I could handle not talking to him every day. Besides, his good morning texts are sometimes the only reason I get to work on time."

Closing her eyes, she felt a tear trickle from the corner of her eyelid. Cursing this new emotional awakening she had found, she brushed it away. "Dad—well, I don't know if Dad has been up here, but I think Dad is ready for something new. Mom, I think you would want that for him, wouldn't you?" She laughed as she exhaled. "Of course you would. You wanted the best for all of us." She could feel the cold metal of the necklace under her shirt.

She remembered her mom lying in the hospital bed the day she died, her body pale and so frail from fighting against the cancer that would take her life. It was a heartbreaking sight, and her mother's soft voice barely spoke above the noise of the machines in the room. Despite her weakened state, her mother had slipped the gold necklace into her hand. The necklace was so big compared to the tiny fingers of a six-year-old, but she gripped it tightly, looking at her mother with tear-soaked eyes.

"Life is beautiful Samantha, an ever-changing adventure that you must be brave for," her mother had whispered. Samantha had shaken her head, eager to please her mom. "Dragonflies have an extra set of wings. Did you know that, Sam?" her mother had asked, looking down at their joined hands. "So, angels can ride on their backs." Sam had stared at the necklace, at the ornate dragonfly sitting in the middle of the gold circle. "When you see one, you'll know that an angel from heaven is visiting you." Her mother had coughed, sputtering beside her and her father had pulled her away, grasping his mother's hand one last time as Sam watched quietly beside her brothers as she took her last breath.

Sam gulped, tears softly falling on her cheek as she brushed them away. "I think Dad's gonna be alright, Mom," she said, her voice trembling. "We all will. I promise."

She stood up to leave, walking toward her car. But before she could go, she glanced back at the stone, and her eyes stopped on a tiny insect hovering over her mother's name. It was a bright blue and green dragonfly, dancing idly around the tombstone. A warm smile brightened Sam's face as she looked up at the sky. "I love you too, Mom," she whispered, and then turned and walked away.

Sam sat on the couch, her leg bouncing nervously as she waited for her family to arrive for the meeting she had called. Already, her suitcases were packed in the back of her VW bug, ready for the road once she knew her family was settled.

Jax was the first to arrive. His steps were still more timid than his usual gait, but she was impressed with the progress he had made. "Look at you, walking around without your walker," she praised him.

"It kept getting stuck in the grass, so I threw it in the trash," he grumbled.

Unsurprised by his comment, she shook her head. "Of course you did."

Her father's heavy footsteps came down the stairs as he kissed her forehead and took a seat on the couch. "Did I hear you making a racket in your room last night?" he asked.

"Oh, um, yeah. We'll talk about it later," she said nonchalantly, exchanging a glance with her brother.

Dylan burst through the front door. "Sorry, didn't mean to be late, had to put up a sign to say that the shop would be open late this morning."

He hopped over the back of the couch and plopped down next to her, earning a grumble from their father. "Raised in a barn, I swear."

"Alright, I think this Lancaster meeting can officially begin," Sam said, standing up. "I called you all here today because Dad has an announcement to make."

Her father stared at her wide-eyed. "Sam!"

"Everyone here, except for Dylan, already knows at least part of what is going on, so we need to get this out in the open," she stated clearly, causing Dylan to look around the room as if offended to be the last one in on the secret. Her dad exhaled in resignation.

"Fine, I've been talking to some investors in Erie about selling the shop."

"What?" Dylan's eyes grew three times bigger.

Jax interjected, "Which is what caused our argument the night of my accident!"

"I fucking knew it," Dylan said.

"Okay, everyone, take a step back," Sam said, raising her voice. "Dad, tell everyone *why* you want to sell the shop."

As he searched her eyes, she nodded in support, urging him to continue. "Long before you kids, I always wanted to travel. But after I met your mom, once we had Jax, there was nothing that was taking me away from here, from our home. I have no regrets about that decision. Please never doubt that." Her dad's voice resonated with conviction. "I love your mom, and I would do anything for her, but perhaps the time has come for me to pursue something that is solely for me."

"Dad, if you felt this way, why didn't you just tell us?" Jax asked, his tone tinged with frustration.

"I wanted to leave you guys the cash from the shop so that you could follow your own dreams without feeling tied down to the life I built here," he said.

Jax grumbled, "You could have simply asked. The life you created, the life we shared, became my dream, Dad. By giving it away without considering what it meant to us, it felt like you didn't believe any of us were deserving of what you had built."

"No, Jax, that wasn't my intention at all." Their dad's sincerity was palpable. "I never wanted you to feel unworthy. You have always managed the shop better than I have, and Dylan has stepped up and worked his ass off while you were in the hospital." Her dad groaned and ran his hand through his hair. "Let's be honest, I haven't been the best dad I could be once your mom passed on."

Jax stared at him wide-eyed. "What are you talking about?"

To her amazement, she watched as a tear formed in the corner of her father's eye, something she had never seen before in her entire life. He squeezed his eyes shut, quickly brushing it away, and confessed, "I couldn't be there for you like she could."

"Dad, you have always been there for us," Jax tried to reassure him. "You've been our rock."

Their dad seemed genuinely concerned that he had somehow screwed up their lives. "I should have done more. Mary would have hugged you when you skinned your knee. She would have taught you how to deal with your emotions instead of punching your way out of them. She would never have been the reason that one of you ended up in the hospital."

Sam knew in her heart that none of that was true and felt the need for her dad to hear her. "The way you raised us, right, wrong, none of that matters. You raised us to be Lancasters, and we are all proud of that," she said.

"Hell yeah," Dylan said proudly beside her.

She added, "Sure, I learned not to cry when I skinned my knee, and you may not have hugged me after, but I always knew that you'd be there to buy me a lollipop and ruffle my hair, and that was just as good as a hug in my book."

Dylan chuckled. "And I would probably still punch my way out of a fight, even if Mom was still around. I'd probably just get grounded for it. At least I learned how to stick up for myself because of you."

Jax shifted in his seat. "I caused my accident, Dad, not you. I was distracted. I knew better than to be driving up there in that state, and I did it anyway. That's on me, Dad, not you."

Their father sighed. "Mary loved you kids so much. All she wanted when she left this world was for you to be taken care of."

Looking around the room at her brothers, she reassured her father, "And we are all fine, Dad. Maybe we aren't perfect, but we're survivors, just like you." She paused. "And we are adults, capable of taking care of ourselves, so maybe it's time you do the same."

Their father responded solemnly, "I can't just leave the shop and run out of town. That's my responsibility."

"Then let me take over. I'll buy the shop," Jax said.

His dad looked at him, a glimmer of hope in his eyes. "You would want that?" he asked with genuine curiosity.

Jax shook his head. "Lancaster's is our family legacy. We built that together. I'm good at it, and let's face it, I ain't good at much else."

"You know I'll be here to help out, too," Dylan said.

Jax shook his head again, expressing his doubt. "Only until you decide you want something else. I know this isn't what you want out of life, Dyl."

Dylan shrugged. "Well, it's not like anything else has come calling."

"You know I'll have you until you run off like Sam did," Jax said.

"Speaking of running off—" Sam looked sheepish. "Might be as good as time as any to tell you all that I'm going to head back to Pittsburgh."

Dylan narrowed his eyes. "When?"

Sam responded with a timid grin, "I was thinking after we solved this whole Lancaster Auto Shop situation."

Jax couldn't hide his surprise, exclaiming loudly, "Today? But next week is Christmas."

Sam tried to explain. "I know, I know. I said I would stay 'til after the holidays, but things have, uh, come up and I need to go back." She nervously pulled a strand of her hair free from her messy bun, causing both of her brothers to exchange suspicious glances.

Jax probed, "Things have come up?"

Sam replied, shaking her head, "Yeah, just some, uh, stuff I need to take care of. Nothing terribly important, just stuff."

Dylan crossed his arms over his chest, visibly frustrated. "Whose ass am I kicking now?"

Their father interjected, stating flatly, "I think you've done enough ass-kicking for the entire family, son. If your sister says she needs to go home, then we listen to her."

Both brothers reluctantly accepted, whining in unison, "Fine."

Dylan concluded with a huff, "But I reserve the ass-kicking option if I hear anything later."

She stood up, looking around the room. "So, it sounds like you guys have a plan here?"

The men all nodded in agreement. "I think we have some things to talk about, but yeah, I think Lancaster's Auto Shop will continue on in the right hands," her father said, nodding at Jax.

"Then I call this meeting to an end," she announced happily.

Dylan stood, and she wrapped her arms around his neck, suddenly sad as he embraced her. She didn't realize how much she would miss him. "What aren't you telling me, sis?" he whispered in her ear.

She patted his back. "We'll talk before I head out, alright?" He nodded and released her.

She then wrapped her arms around Jax's waist, unable to reach his neck. "Don't slack off on your exercises. I know how stubborn you are," she said.

An exasperated look crossed his face. "Who's stubborn?" he asked.

"Whatever. Try to stay in touch this time. Phones work both ways," she lectured him.

"Try visiting more often. Cars drive both ways," he said.

"Touché, brother!" she said with a wink.

Walking over to her dad, she opened her arms and wrapped them around him. "I'll miss you, Daddy. Make sure you let me know once you have your plans set," she said.

He wrapped his hands in her hair at the base of her neck and tugged her closer. "Thank you for everything, Dragonfly."

"Mom says everything is going to be alright," she whispered. "Life is an ever-changing adventure that you must be brave for, remember?"

For the second time that day, she saw a tear welling in his eye as his hands cupped her face. "Never let go, kid," he said, hugging her again.

"Not on your life." She grinned, hugging him tightly one more time.

Chapter Twenty-Four

Blake

Blake

Hey, I know you are still probably pissed about the fight

Blake

But theres something I need to tell you

Blake

We really need to talk

Blake

Can you just text me back

Blake

Please?

He knew Sam was likely pissed off about walking in on the fight between him, Dylan, and Casey. However, it wasn't like her to completely ghost him. Since walking into the bar and seeing him get whisked away in handcuffs, she had gone radio silent. Admittedly, it wasn't his best moment, but he would rather she just yell at him and get it over with instead of this silent treatment. He didn't know what she was thinking at all.

On top of that, he needed to tell her he was in love with her. Clearly, the timing was bad. None of this was lost on him; however, timing wasn't exactly on his side either. Jax was getting better. Christmas was approaching, and Sam would be returning to Pittsburgh before he knew it. If he didn't tell her, he would regret it for the rest of his life.

If only she would answer her damn phone.

He stood in front of his mirror, leaning toward it as he turned his head from side to side, examining the deep purple bruises on his face. He really had been behaving like a juvenile lately. Standing up taller, he brushed his hand through his messy hair.

"Sam, there's something I've been meaning to tell you for weeks." He grumbled incoherently under his breath and started over. "Samantha, I may not have recognized your beauty when we were younger, but..."

No, that wasn't right. She was always beautiful; he was just an idiot for looking past it. He readjusted his shirt and began again.

"Sam, these last few months have meant more to me than I can even explain," he said, groaning audibly, howling at the mirror image of himself. "Hell, I love you! I love you and I can't live another day without telling you that."

"You should have just started with that one." He jumped at the sound of his sister's voice as she leaned against the door frame, a knowing smile on her face.

"Goddamnit, Kels, try knocking next time," he growled anxiously.

"And miss the show? No thanks," she said, crossing her arms in front of her. "Don't stop on my account. You were just getting to the good stuff."

Glancing toward the ceiling in frustration, he fell back onto his bed. "None of it sounds important enough," he groaned, exhaling loudly.

"Sounded pretty important to me," she said sincerely.

"The words don't mean enough, you know. It's not impactful or a big enough gesture." He sighed. "It's like the end of those big romantic movies you hate so much, but always seem to be watching. The guy always says something impactful and incredibly cheesy, and the girl throws herself in his arms and—"

She interrupted with a snort, yet her voice was sincere. "Yeah, I get it. They live happily ever after and wash, rinse, repeat." She sat down on the bed next to him. "This isn't a movie, Blake. And you are definitely not some handsome, strapping stud who's racing through the airport to win the heart of the plucky heroine."

He glanced in the mirror, taking offense. "Hey, I'm not bad looking."

She shrugged. "Yeah, I'm sure girls aren't disgusted by you, but we are getting away from the point here." Grumbling, he looked away. "Sam isn't the type of girl who wants flowery words and overly impressive gestures. The words themselves don't actually matter, Blake."

Snorting, he replied, "Of course they matter, Kels. It's not like I'm going to run up to her and yell random crap at her like I'm some prehistoric caveman, and she's just going to fall at my feet."

"Would you stop being obstinate and actually listen to me for once?" She lectured. "You're performing, and you don't need to. Sam Lancaster has looked at you like you hung the moon for years. You could trip and fall on your face while simply saying 'I love you,' and I think she would find it to be the most romantic thing you ever did." She leaned over and kissed his forehead before heading for the door. "Just be yourself, dumbass," she said with a shrug. "I'm gonna head to the diner for a bit. Enjoy your day off and try not to get into any more fights," she added cheekily. "You might not be ugly, but your face is starting to look like a punching bag."

His smile was sincere as he watched her, leaving him alone in silence to contemplate her words. Maybe it was as simple as just telling Sam how he felt without some romantic gesture. He loved her, something that felt incredibly important to him all on its own. Blake had never been in love before. Beyond his mother and sister, no one had ever mattered to him as much as Sam Lancaster, and now he'd do anything for her. It was terrifying not knowing how she felt in return.

He knew Sam had a crush on him, but love, the only person who could know that for sure, was Sam.

Maybe his sister was right. Maybe he didn't need to have the right words; he just needed to speak to her from his heart.

Now, he just needed her to actually be willing to talk to him.

Chapter Twenty-Five

Samantha

Sam shoved her phone in her pocket, purposely ignoring Blake's message. She knew exactly what he wanted to talk about, and although it might have seemed cowardly, she didn't have the courage to face him when he inevitably told her about giving it another try with Donna. Admittedly, she understood that her decision to ghost him and run was foolish and immature. At twenty-six years old, she should have been able to handle rejection. Besides, they weren't even dating or exclusive. Their relationship had merely been a casual fling while she was in town, and now that she was leaving today, it was over anyway. In her mind, she owed him nothing.

Determined to move on, Sam had already made a mental note to block Donna on Instagram as soon as she returned to Pittsburgh.

She couldn't bear to see pictures of them together. It might sting more than she was prepared to deal with now that she was in this new emotional exploratory phase of her life.

As she stepped onto the porch, she noticed Dylan waiting by her car. Letting out a heavy sigh, she reluctantly walked toward him, dodging Whiskey as he jumped around her legs before she bent down and gave him a pat goodbye on the head. "You gonna tell me what has you running out of here with your tail between your legs?"

"I thought you were going to be less protective," she said.

Dylan's lips pursed tightly together as he contemplated her response. "That depends—why aren't you saying goodbye to Blake all of a sudden?" he asked.

With a tight smile on her face, Sam leaned against the driver's side door of the car and stared down at her feet. "Go easy on him. I think we just live in two different worlds and maybe we want different things," she said sadly.

Dylan started to disagree. "That doesn't sound like the Blake I know."

Sam interrupted, her voice heavy with resignation, "Well, maybe he isn't the person I thought he was either. In any case, I can't keep living in a fantasy. Dad's out there searching for his second chance, and maybe it's time I start living my own life. None of us are getting any younger, Dyl," she said, her thoughts filled with a mixture of determination and uncertainty as she spoke.

Confused, Dylan responded. "I guess I just don't know what changed."

Sam shrugged. "Me neither, but it doesn't really matter. He's happy with his life here and the people in it, and I have to respect that," she said wistfully.

Dylan objected, but Sam interrupted, "I love you, Dyl. Let me live my life, alright?" They shared a tight hug. "And I do expect that you will text me every morning. Otherwise, I'll probably get fired for being late to work."

He laughed, leaning forward to hug her tightly. "Maybe I'll come see you next time, since you refuse to come visit enough."

She added softly, "I'd like that." Deep down, she knew she would miss him the most.

Driving out of town, she passed by the diner and saw Kelley standing out back, cigarette in her hand. She pulled over and parked her car. Stepping onto the curb, she called out, "I told you those things will kill you."

Kelley looked up and smiled. "Hey, Sam. Blake's not here today."

Sam breathed a sigh of relief. "I actually stopped by to see you."

The girl smiled and put out her cigarette with her shoe. "Oh, everything okay? How's Dylan's face?"

She laughed. "I actually think it made some improvements. He looks more distinguished with purple bruises. Might have even straightened his nose." They shared a giddy laugh.

Kelley shook her head as she remarked, "Blake looks like shit."

There was an awkward silence until Sam broke it. "I, uh, I came over to say goodbye, actually."

Kelley looked shocked and leaned against the diner. "Goodbye?"

Sam took a deep breath. "Yeah, I'm headed back to Pittsburgh today. Actually, I was on my way out of town when I saw you outside and stopped," she continued. "Jax is walking really well now and doesn't really need my help. It just makes sense for me to get back."

Kelley blurted anxiously, "I thought you were staying for Christmas."

"Dylan has things under control here, so it didn't seem necessary for me to stick around," she said. "Besides, my dad is looking to get started on a trip right after the holidays. He's actually planning to stop by my place before he goes."

The girl looked confused, and Sam couldn't bear to see the sadness on her face. "When I moved out-of-town four years ago," she began. "I had this idea that I was 'embarking on a great adventure' to find myself."

Kelley snorted and remarked, "Is that something people actually do?"

She shrugged. "Maybe it's just a concept found in self-help books. Personally, I've never made it through an entire one." Reflecting on her recent experiences, Sam said, "I believe that over the past few months, I've truly learned a lot about myself. I've discovered who I am, and I think I might be ready for something more in my life."

Kelley excitedly responded, "That's great! So why are you leaving? What about Blake?"

Sam smiled. "You're a good kid, Kelley. My advice is to go to Berkeley. Don't wait for Blake to make his move. Don't worry about your mom; she'll be fine. You need to find your dream, your big adventure, and go live it. Don't have any regrets."

As Sam backed away from the diner wall and started walking toward the car, she turned back and waved. "Tell Blake that I genuinely hope he and Donna make it work this time."

Kelley shook her head, a look of confusion on her face as she frowned and raised her hand in a half wave goodbye.

While driving through town, she turned on her radio just as The Foo Fighters' song "Home" came on. Instantly, she cranked up the volume and sped up her vehicle, settling in for the two-hour drive back to the city.

As the town faded away in the rear-view mirror, her thoughts drifted to the last few months. Initially, when Donna drove a stake through her heart by revealing that she and Blake were deciding to work things out, she had been utterly crushed, her heart shattered on the floor.

However, as the town disappeared behind her, she began reflecting on the remarkable transformation she had undergone since returning.

When she had arrived back in October, filled with fear for her brother's condition and unsure of what awaited her, she thought she would be here to help her brother to heal physically. Little did she expect this journey would also heal her emotionally.

She had survived for years, with an attitude of being untouchable. Nothing penetrated her shell. When it came to relationships, she erected a protective wall around her heart, effectively shielding herself from potential pain.

Unfortunately, this self-preservation also meant denying herself the opportunity to experience the profound connection she had with Blake. The truth was, she felt an overwhelming and unexpected depth of emotion with him. Perhaps the risk of a broken heart was worth the reward of the embrace of love.

She realized that what she had discovered with Blake was something she yearned for in her own life: love. And now, she had no desire to extinguish that flame once again.

She might be returning to Pittsburgh licking her wounds, but she was returning a brand-new woman, open and willing to experience new things.

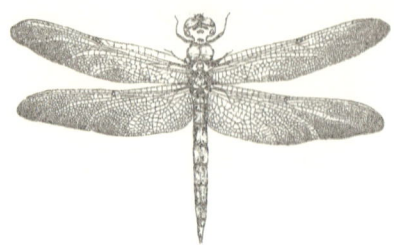

Chapter Twenty-Six

Blake

Blake sat at the kitchen table, engrossed in his lunch. As he tapped on his phone, his attention was divided between his meal and the text messages he had sent to Sam. However, frustration crept in when he noticed she had read his message hours ago without responding. The lack of any attempted reply only intensified his annoyance.

He was getting incredibly frustrated. He had spent most of his afternoon thinking about his future. His future with Sam, his dream of being a chef, the scholarship sitting on his desk that he had yet to decline. He had realized that maybe taking chances wasn't just about opening your heart to someone and hoping they returned your feelings. Maybe taking chances was about putting yourself out there and following your dreams, even at the risk of failure.

Suddenly, the screen door squeaked, and the front door slammed open, jolting Blake out of his irritation. Standing in the doorway was his sister Kelley, who seemed out of breath. "What the hell are you doing home? Who is watching the diner?"

"I closed the diner," Kelley said, causing Blake to snap to attention.

He couldn't fathom why she would do something so irresponsible. His disapproval was dripping from his response. "You did what? Why would you do that?"

Kelley, however, was in no mood for an argument. She raised her voice. "Shut up and listen to me," she yelled, making Blake pause and focus on what she had to say. "Sam is leaving," Kelley said, her statement dropping like a bomb.

Confused and anxious, Blake demanded clarification. "Leaving? Leaving to where?" he asked.

"Back to Pittsburgh," Kelley said, her words filled with urgency.

The gravity of the situation hit Blake like a ton of bricks, prompting him to reach for his phone and dial Sam's number. As he listened to the ringing on the other end, his heart raced in his chest.

"You've reached Sam. If you're hearing this, I probably don't want to talk to you. Or I'm in the bathroom. Or I'm running a marathon. I'll let you decide." He hung up the call, feeling a surge of panic. Grabbing his jacket, he prepared to leave in a hurry, desperate to catch Sam before she left.

Kelley's unexpected question caught him off guard as he made his way toward the door. "Did you and Donna get back together?" she asked.

Blake's wide-eyed look of horror spoke volumes. "Why the hell would you ask that?"

"Because Sam seems to think you two are working things out." He shook his head in denial. "Well, thank God for that because I was coming over here to tell you what an idiot you were," Kelley said, her frustration dissipating.

"I was just rehearsing how to tell her I loved her. Why on earth would she think I'm getting back together with Donna?" he asked, his voice filled with equal parts confusion and desperation.

Kelley demanded, "I don't know, but you damn well better fix this. She's the best thing that's ever happened to you."

"I'm trying," he said anxiously. "Do you know where she is?"

As he headed out the door and raced to his bike, she yelled, "You aren't going to catch her on that! She was on her way out of town before I even got back into the diner, and then I ran all the way home."

Shaking his head in despair, he realized that his mother had the car at the store and wouldn't be home for hours. Realizing he had no other option, he closed his eyes, shoved past his sister, and ran up the stairs, storming into his room. Standing in front of his dresser, he stared at the box with his father's initials. "Well, Dad, it all comes down to this, doesn't it?" he said softly. "Either I face my demons, or I lose the girl."

Cautiously, he opened the lid and removed the keys from inside. The keys only came out once a month when he used them to start the car to keep it in running condition. Holding them in his hand, he knew what his dad would want him to do. It was the only decision to make. It was the one that required courage, and honestly, Sam was worth it.

"You always liked Sam, didn't you, Dad?" He gripped the keys, remembering how close his father had been with the Lancaster family. "I'm pretty sure she'd say something about me being a pansy right now, so I think it's about time I man up and drive that car, don't you think?"

He ran back down the stairs, past his sister, and headed outside to the garage. Kelley yelled after him, "Where are you going?"

He replied, "To get Sam back." He shoved the garage door upward over his head, causing the scraping sound of metal to squeal in their ears.

They both stood in front of the garage, with the sun shining through, lighting the car in a warm glow. Running his hands over the dusty black GT Mustang, he was engrossed in the way it felt as his hands opened the door.

The memories of his father flooded him, and the smell of the red leather interior invaded his nostrils. Putting the key in the ignition, he smiled as AC/DC's "Thunderstruck" started playing on the radio, accompanied by the thumping of the drums that vibrated inside the vehicle.

He felt a small smile form as it upturned on the corner of his mouth. He watched his sister smiling back at him outside the garage. She stepped to the side as he took in a deep breath. "Okay, Dad. Let's go find Sam."

The car drove with a sense of purpose, responding effortlessly to his foot on the accelerator. He took a shortcut through town, hoping that he could catch her before she got to the freeway, praying that Sheriff Draper's attention was elsewhere as he sped through the town's streets, disobeying every traffic rule in town.

As he turned left, he screeched to a halt when he saw a trail of ducks slowly crossing the road. He gave Mrs. Hattie an anxious smile, and she waved at him, stopping traffic in both directions to allow the small family to waddle happily across the road. His knee bounced nervously against the steering wheel as he rehearsed what he would say to Sam once he found her, hoping he wouldn't be too late. After the last feathered duckling had hopped to safety, he waved to Mrs. Hattie and slowly let his car drift away from the scene before speeding off toward the edge of town.

The old bridge was up ahead, and he knew if he didn't find her soon, that she was most likely already comfortably on her way to the city. He would have to pull over and text Dylan to get her address in Pittsburgh. There was no way he was letting her get away without at least clearing up the misunderstanding. She needed to know how he felt.

With the bridge in sight, a flash of yellow caught his attention—Sam's VW. His heart raced as he pressed harder on the accelerator, determined to catch up with her. Finally spotting her, he honked his horn, hoping not to startle her.

She seemed oblivious, so he honked again. This time, he noticed her brake lights and flashed his headlights, hoping she would pull over. After a few more flashes, she seemed to understand and stopped just before reaching the bridge. He followed suit, pulling over behind her, turning off the car and stepping out.

She was climbing out of her car just ahead of him and he saw a look of surprise register on her face. "Blake? What are you doing?" He approached her slowly, his heart pounding.

"Sam, I uh—" She glanced at his car behind him and furrowed her brow. "I had to see you..." He approached her with caution, wanting nothing more than to pull her into his arms and beg her not to leave, but also not wanting to scare her away, either.

"You could've just texted me, you know," she interrupted with a scowl on her face. This reaction probably didn't bode well for the rest of the conversation.

"Well, you weren't exactly responding to me," he cut her off with a shrug.

Her narrowed eyes and pinched lips most likely weren't a good sign either. "Listen Blake, I understand. I mean, we never defined what this was between us, so you don't owe me any explanations. Besides, Donna informed me, so this all seems..."

His head jerked back in confusion. "Informed you of what, exactly?"

As he watched her blow a strand of hair away from her face, she stared back at him. "About the two of you working things out. And I get it, I—"

He closed his eyes and exhaled a frustrated snort. "Sam, I have no idea what you're talking about." She blinked back at him. "I've been driving myself crazy since I got thrown in jail, maybe even before that, trying to figure out how to tell you I'm in love with you. So, whatever Donna said, it's complete and utter bullshit. None of it is true."

"Wait, what?" she exclaimed, tilting her head as she stared back at him, blinking rapidly. "What did you say?"

"I said it's bullshit," he repeated, his tone firm as he crossed his arms against his chest. He couldn't believe that Donna was once again messing up his life with her crap.

"Not that part," she said, shaking her head, her chest rising and falling rapidly. "You're in love with me?" She appeared stunned, and after a moment, his brain finally caught up with him.

Relief washed over him as his smile grew wide. "Madly," he confessed, stepping closer to her. "Wildly."

She flinched, uncertainty flickering in her eyes. "But—" she protested. "Donna, and Pittsburgh and—"

Before she could finish, he reached for her and gently touched her cheek. "I love you, Samantha Lancaster."

In the end, he realized he didn't need a grand monologue or prepared speech. It was as if his eyes told a story that only she could read. She pushed up on her toes, wrapping her arms around his neck, her fingers diving into his hair. Their lips crashed into each other in a passionate kiss that was just as good, if not better, than the climax of any romantic movie he had ever watched. He pulled her closer, his arms encircling her waist, wishing they could stay like this forever.

But Blake knew this wasn't the movies, because if it was, the credits would be rolling and the screen would fade to black. The movies never dealt with what happened next and all the problems just rolled into the happily ever after that the audience never got to see.

He pulled away slightly, gazing into her green eyes. "I'm sorry this got all messed up," he said. "And I know we have a lot to discuss, because obviously none of this is simple or easy."

"It's not. There is so much we have to talk about." She bit her lip, and he felt that nervous energy building inside of him again.

"I know, and I want to talk about it," he said nervously. "When you didn't respond to my messages, I kind of spiraled," he said. "And if you don't feel the same way about—"

She touched her fingers to his lips, silencing him. "I love you, Blake," she said, her words filled with sincerity. Those were the best words he had ever heard spoken to him. "I'm sorry I didn't respond to your text messages."

"I'm sorry Donna tried to ruin my life again." He laughed, bending down to touch his lips to hers once more. "I just couldn't let you leave without knowing the truth about how I felt about you."

"I wanted to tell you so many times. I came to your house after your arrest. That's when I saw Donna." He thought back to Donna being at his house after he had gotten home after his arrest. The day he clarified in no uncertain terms that they were over, and the pieces fell into place.

He wrapped his arms tighter around her. "She had stopped by with the same manipulation tactics again and I had just told her I was never getting back with her because I was in love with you."

Sam sighed, a soft curse whispered under her breath. "I'm an idiot."

"Nah," he reassured her, "she's just great at what she does. Trust me, I've fallen victim to it for years." He scrunched his face, and the corner of his lips turned up into a smile. "Which *we* will never fall for again," he added with swift determination.

"So, now what?" she asked, looking back at her car with a frown. "I really am going back to Pittsburgh," she said sadly.

He bit the corner of his lip and sighed. "I know. You live there, after all." He looked back at his car and added, "But I can come visit you now."

She leaned against him, kissed his cheek, and whispered, "Nice wheels, by the way, Forrester. Very sexy."

He pulled her against him, running his hands along her arm. "My girlfriend told me I should just drive the damn car, and well, my dad would have wanted me to be able to go visit her."

She stared at him in amusement, her eyes wide. "Girlfriend?"

He shrugged, rubbing the back of his neck nervously. "I guess I was kinda hoping she would want to be."

She tucked into his arm, snuggling against him. "I thought you'd never ask."

He kissed her forehead and sighed. "But uh, the visits might take a little while."

"Blake, I understand you not wanting to leave the diner often—"

He placed his finger against her soft lips, shaking his head, and interrupted, "Actually, I made a few phone calls this morning and I'm kinda moving to New York." He let his confession hang in the air as she took in his words.

"What? Are you serious? You're really going to do it?" she said, jumping up and hugging him around the neck until he was choking for air.

"I can't breathe, Sam." He chuckled. "But yeah, I'm taking the scholarship and going to culinary school."

"I'm so proud of you." She smiled. "You're going to be an amazing chef."

"Thanks, Sam, you know, for pushing me into the uncomfortable," he said as she put her palm into his and squeezed. They stood there, leaning against her car and staring off into the forest. He could tell she had gotten lost in her thoughts, and it was on the tip of his tongue to ask her where she had gone before she was speaking again.

"Are you sure we can do this?" she asked. "It's a lot of change, all at once. New York, Pittsburgh, a relationship, long distance. It all seems so..."

Her voice trailed off as Blake looked down at her, his finger gently sliding along her chin. Tilting her face up to meet his eyes, he watched her eyes dance with uncertainty. "You're worth it to me, Samantha Lancaster." A warm smile accompanied his misty-eyed declaration, prompting her own eyes to widen in response. "If I have to call you every day, send goofy texts, or silly selfies just to remind you of my face, I'll do it. Whatever it takes," he pledged, planting a soft kiss on her lips before resting his forehead against hers. "You want me to wear an 'I love Sam Lancaster' T-shirt? Cause I'll do that too." She giggled and playfully slapped his chest. "I'm not joking, I bet Kelley will make me one with Mom's Cricut machine."

"I can't believe this is real," she whispered, snuggling into his chest.

"Does this not feel real?" He kissed her forehead, then pressed his lips against her temples. "Or this?"

"You don't understand, Blake. I used to lie in bed at night, staring out my window, hoping to see a shooting star just so I could make a wish," she said. "Every single shooting star I ever saw growing up, I always wished for the same thing."

"What did you wish for?" She glanced up at him and their eyes met, and his heart suddenly sped up, already knowing her answer.

"You. I wished for you, Blake."

He swallowed, blinking. "I'm sorry I didn't see you back then." His lips pressed into her hair. "Not that I didn't see you, I just—not like this. If I could change it, if I could see you sooner..."

When she looked up, her eyes were glassy, catching him off guard. Sam Lancaster had never been an emotional girl growing up, not in the way he was used to with other girls. However, the way she looked at him now made him feel special, as if this was something new and treasured between them.

"I think things happened exactly how they were supposed to, Blake," she said.

"You think so?" he asked as he brushed one of her curls out of her face and lightly traced his thumb across her cheek. He had no idea how he had gotten so lucky.

"Definitely. Everything in life happens for a reason, at the exact time it's supposed to happen. It's an ever-changing adventure that you must be brave for," she mused softly, mostly to herself. "I think I'm ready for it." She looked up into his eyes. "I'm definitely ready for you."

"Oh yeah, well, I'm more than ready for you, Samantha Lancaster?" he said with a soft grin and a wink. "But you had better get on the road before I pull you into the backseat of that Mustang and have my way with you."

She peered around him, staring at his car with a raised brow as she replied, "Don't tempt me with a good time, Forrester."

And if they spent another hour making out on the side of the road by the old county bridge in the backseat of that Mustang, well, who was going to tell? And as Blake watched her pull away in that yellow VW bug, as the sun was setting in the distance, she stared back at him with a soft smile and a small wave. He knew that although Pittsburg and New York were big steps and new challenges in front of them; they were more than ready for whatever adventure was about to come their way.

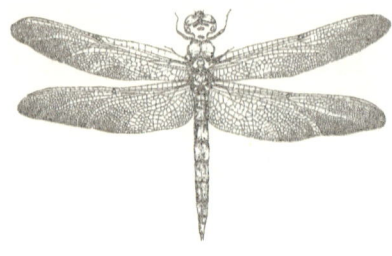

Epilogue

Samantha

Six months later...

"Blake, did you see where that box labeled office went?" Sam called him from the bedroom as Blake unpacked a box in the kitchen.

Responding, he yelled back, "I think I saw it in the living room. It's behind the couch."

Sam, with messy hair stuck to her forehead and sweat on her brow, appeared from the hallway. Meanwhile, Blake stood there, looking like a picture of male perfection. "Where?" she asked with a laugh.

"What have you been doing?" Confused, he wrapped his arms around her back as he pulled her closer. "You look like you've been running laps, but my girl doesn't exercise, so I know that's not it." He playfully pecked his lips against her mouth. "And I know we have had no extracurricular activity today, so it's not that."

"Does moving make you horny?" she swatted his chest.

"Not particularly, no," he said. Sam glanced around at the mess of boxes in their new apartment in New York and then looked up at him. "My girlfriend, on the other hand, does a little something for me." She giggled loudly, her head falling backward as he tickled her neck with his mouth.

"Blake, stop, I mean it. I need to find that box," she said, breaking their playful moment. "It has my camera and my portfolio in it. I have a meeting with the Yankees tomorrow about my start date and I need to bring that stuff with me." He placed another kiss on her cheek and went in search of the box, disappearing into the other room. Sam watched him go, admiring his ass as he walked. She truly was a lucky woman.

It was hard to explain how quickly her life had changed. One moment, Blake Forrester kissed her on the road leading out of Titusville, and the next, she was changing her entire life.

She had gone back to Pittsburgh and talked to her boss about potentially changing venues. She was fortunate to have a great contact with the Yankees who had been hounding her for months to come work with them in New York. Sam had always been reluctant to move teams, preferring to stay close to home. However, with Blake moving to New York, this presented the perfect opportunity for her to make the move.

Just then, there was a knock on the front door, and Sam went down the hall to answer it. "Did you order something?" she hollered in the direction he had disappeared.

"Nope," came his response.

Opening the door, she found a short, dark-haired woman and a tall, gorgeous supermodel. "Hi!" exclaimed the younger one. "I'm Lucy, and this is my sister Amber. We're your neighbors in 12-C."

Blake jogged up behind her, carrying the box she had been looking for. "Found the box you—Oh, hey!" he said, noticing they had guests.

Sam smiled and turned toward Blake. "Blake, this is Lucy and her sister Amber. They're our neighbors."

He adjusted the box in his grasp and offered his hand. "Nice to meet you both. Sam and I just moved here from Pennsylvania."

"Oh, exciting," Lucy squealed. "I love meeting new people."

"Sorry, my kid sister gets happy about pretty much everything," Amber added, glancing down at her perfectly manicured nails.

"We like to organize potlucks for the building and host parties on the roof," Lucy said.

"*You* like to do that," Amber corrected. "I get roped into helping out, but let's be clear, I don't enjoy it." She grinned sarcastically.

"Well, anyway, it's a fun way to get to know your neighbors." She handed her a pamphlet. "We're doing one next week if you both want to come."

Blake grabbed the paper over her shoulder. "Sounds fun. I'm in cooking school, so might be a good way to practice some recipes I've learned."

Sam grinned up at Blake. Ever since he had started the Culinary Institute, he had been excited to test out everything he had learned at school, and she was his eager guinea pig. He would stop at the store for new ingredients each week, delighting her with exciting dishes to taste and explore.

"OH!" Lucy bounced excitedly. "A chef at our parties. People are going to be so excited."

"Yeah well, let's leave them be shall we Luce," Amber said. "Sorry about her. She really is a ray of fucking sunshine all the time. If you're ever depressed, just come visit. She'll perk you right up."

Amber turned, spinning around on her five-inch heels, and Sam couldn't help but notice her toned calves. Just what she needed: a hot Amazonian princess in the building. "It was nice meeting you both," Lucy said sincerely. "If you need anything at all, just let me know."

"Thanks, Lucy, I'll remember that."

With a smile, Sam closed the door and looked up at Blake. "They were interesting," he said with a laugh.

Sam snorted and replied, "You mean the tall one was hot?"

"That wasn't what I meant at all," he defended. "Besides, I already have a hot girlfriend right here." The kiss was slow at first, building as he set the box on the table in the hallway. He walked her backward toward the bedroom just as her phone rang. "Ignore it," he urged.

"It might be my dad." She grinned into his kiss. She slipped out of his arms and rushed toward her phone. Sure enough, it was her father on the other end. "Hey, Daddy," she answered excitedly, putting him on speakerphone. "Where are you at now?"

"Hi, Dragonfly. I just stopped in Utah and thought I would give you guys a call and check in." Her father's voice was a welcome sound. He called her at least twice a week to make sure she was doing alright and to update her on his latest adventures on the road.

"How's Blake?" he asked.

"Hey, Mr. Lancaster," Blake yelled as he came back down the hallway.

"Tell that boy to stop calling me that," her father scolded. "I'm not eighty years old, no matter what the RV implies."

Blake laughed and kissed her forehead as she settled onto the couch with the phone in her hand. "I'll be sure to remind him, Daddy."

"You guys getting settled in?" he asked.

Sam stared at the boxes that threatened to overtake their current room. She didn't remember having this much "stuff" in Pittsburgh when she was living on her own. Yet, here she was, sitting next to a box labeled "Sam's crap," realizing that she might have more than she had originally thought.

"I'm sure we'll be done unpacking in six months," Blake said as he plopped down beside her, pulling her legs into his lap.

He had driven back to Titusville last weekend to load up a U-Haul full of boxes that his mother had set aside for him. Throughout the last week, they went through the boxes after dinner, with the help of a bottle of wine. Among the items were football trophies, old high school yearbooks, and photographs of the two of them throughout the years, which gave them a lot to reminisce about.

Excited to find a stash of Blake's old jerseys in one of the boxes, she was thrilled to have more sleep shirts to add to her collection. However, Blake considered himself the victor in the situation.

After spending months apart and sending dirty text messages and the occasional Facetime desperation sex sessions, Sam had expected that her sex life with Blake would have settled into a relaxed state. However, living together seemed to have had the opposite effect, as it made them more desperate for each other. Blake, for the most part, couldn't keep his hands off of her, and in turn, Sam found herself greedy for him.

"Where are you heading next?" Sam asked, leaning her head back against one of their decorative pillows.

"Think I'm going to spend a few days in Arizona." Her father's voice wavered as if he was walking. "Jax seems to be a bit overwhelmed at the shop. Have you talked to him lately?"

"Not this week. I can call him if you want?" Sam said, giving Blake a concerned glance.

"Probably unnecessary. But I'm going to send him some help anyway," he said, laughing into the other end of the receiver.

"Help? Daddy, what are you doing?" Sam asked.

"Nothing that isn't for his own good. You know your brother. He's stubborn as a mule." Her dad laughed. "Thought he might need some help with the books. I know someone from Erie that can help him out."

"Daddy, you know Jax won't want that," she said.

"Yeah, well, he wouldn't know what he wanted if it slapped him in the face," he said with a chuckle. "This one might, actually."

"Daddy..." Sam warned.

"Don't worry your pretty little head about it, Dragonfly," her dad said, as Blake leaned over to kiss her knee. "You two just focus on your move and getting settled in. I'll check in with you guys next week."

"Bye, Daddy," she sang, bidding him farewell.

"Bye Mister—Ken," Blake corrected as they hung up. "I can't get used to that. It's weird calling him by his first name," he said with a pout.

"You'll get used to it, baby," she said, reassuring him, sitting up and crawling onto his lap.

"Ken Lancaster scares me, Sam," he confessed, looking up at her as she ran her fingers through his hair.

Sam let her lips linger against his ear. "Why don't you focus your energy elsewhere?"

"And where would you like me to focus it?" he asked. She grabbed his hands, pushing them between their bodies, their mouths pressing together as his fingers slid between her legs.

However, their intimate moment was interrupted by her phone vibrating on the couch beside her. "No," she said, groaning as she looked down to see Jax's name pop up on the screen. "It's my brother."

"He's not invited into this," Blake groaned as she leaned over and picked up the phone, putting him on speaker.

"Hey, Jax."

"Sis, who the fuck is Allison Hanover?" Jax said immediately.

"Allison? I don't know. You tell me?" Sam said as Blake played with the ties on her shorts.

"Well, I don't know, and Dad's not talking either," he said.

She asked, "What does Dad have to do with it?"

"I don't know, but she has something to do with that firm in Erie he was talking to." Suddenly, she realized maybe this was the help that her dad was referring to earlier.

"Oh," she said.

Jax asked, "What does 'oh' mean?"

She explained, "It's just that Dad mentioned sending you some help with the books." She could hear his apprehension. "Maybe just keep an open mind, Jax. Dad wouldn't do something if it wasn't beneficial."

"Who are you, and what have you done with my sister?" Jax paused. "Is this how sex warped your brain?"

Blake snorted. "Careful now, I might take offense."

"Sorry, bro, no offense. Didn't realize you were there."

Blake gently kissed her neck, causing Sam to giggle. "Blake is always here," she said.

"Yeah, I'll let you two lovebirds go," Jax chimed in.

"Just be nice to whoever Allison is," Sam said. "Promise me."

Jax agreed. "I'll be as nice as I can be," before hanging up the phone.

Finally alone, Blake tossed the phone to the other end of the couch and pulled Sam closer, grabbing her by the ass as she felt his erection grow.

However, the moment was interrupted by a buzzing sound indicating an incoming text message. Blake shook his head, determined not to let anything distract him. "No, absolutely not. You're mine now," he said.

Just as he said it, his own phone rang. He quickly answered it, only to hear Kelley's voice on the other end. "Did you know that in California, half of the women are either bisexual or gay?" she asked.

Blake chuckled. "I'm pretty sure that's not true, but right now, I'm trying to have sex with Sam. I'll call you later."

Ending the call, he noticed Sam's shocked expression. "You did not just do that!" she said, her voice raising slightly.

Blake playfully tossed her onto her back, hovering over her. "No more interruptions," he growled, ready to continue where they left off.

Sam relished in the sensation of his hands on her hips, his body moving rhythmically against hers as he firmly grasped her legs and pulled them over his shoulders. As he buried his face into her underwear, he hummed softly, smoothly sliding his thumbs into the hem of her cotton panties and effortlessly pulling them down her hips, flinging them across the room. "Hey, you'll have to find those later," she pleaded, but he paid no attention, eagerly delving between her legs with his tongue, expertly finding the perfect spot between her folds that sent waves of pleasure through her body.

Overwhelmed by his touch, she wriggled beneath him; her pleasure building as his fingers skillfully brought her to her peak, his smirk pressed against her thigh as he kissed his way up her leg.

"I never tire of hearing that," he said confidently, causing her to sit up and push him back against the couch.

"Yeah? Do you enjoy it?" she gasped, her voice filled with anticipation. "Tell me, what else do you like?"

As he looked up at her, his eyes dark with desire, the hunger and desperation evident, he swiftly removed his pants from his thigh and discarded them on the ground. The moment was messy and swift as she raised herself and lowered onto his erect member, the sound of their moans reverberating through the sparsely furnished apartment. "God yes, Sam," he groaned, gripping her back tightly.

She watched him intently as she rode him, feeling him fill her completely, her lips slightly parted in ecstasy. "Keep riding me, baby," he encouraged. Their mouths hovered tantalizingly close, barely brushing against each other.

She was close. It wouldn't take long. Blake had a way of getting her there so easily. He brushed against her, gripped her hip. It was hard; it was fast. They were screaming each other's name and then they were panting, staring into each other's eyes. His hands in her hair, whispers of love in her ear. She was lucky beyond all measure.

She fell onto the couch beside him, their naked bodies covered in sweat. She reached for her phone, seeing the texts from Dylan.

Dilly Bear

As soon as Jax has things under control please tell me i can come see you guys

Dilly Bear

Cuz hes driving me crazy

She held her phone over her head, reading her texts. "Dylan wants to come see us soon," she said.

Blake frowned in response. "Not until we're older and stop having sex."

She frowned, looking up at him as he slid closer to her. "You're not going to have sex with me when we're older?" She pouted.

"I'm going to have sex with you until the day we die." He grinned in that devilishly handsome way. "Tell him I said we have a couple of hot neighbors for him to meet."

She argued against it. "I'm not telling him that."

He shrugged. "Suit yourself."

He sat up, pulling his shirt back on over his head. Standing, he made his way back into the kitchen, his naked ass providing the best view she had seen all day. Leaning back against the couch, she couldn't help but reflect on the last few months. Her move to New York, Blake's progress at culinary school, and their growing love for each other. It was remarkable how much had changed in the last year.

She had opened herself up to love, dared to live, and fully embraced her feelings. She no longer suppressed emotion in her life, she now let it guide her. Each new emotion had become a chapter in her story, an integral part of her adventurous journey.

"Hey babe, you okay?" Blake stood at the edge of the couch, staring at her.

She smiled up at him and replied, "I'm wonderful."

He grinned in response. In that moment, as he crossed the room and bent over to kiss her forehead, she saw the boy she had loved for so many years staring back at her. It made her feel like the luckiest girl in the world. "I love you, Sam," he said.

"I love you too, Blake Forrester," she said with a satisfied smile.

Firefly

Book 2 : A Lancaster Novel

Jackson Lancaster might not be the smartest of the Lancaster siblings. Though he will admit he was the slowest since his accident
last year, but there was one thing that he excelled at that neither
his sister Samantha nor his brother Dylan could ever compare. He
could sniff out bullshit from any distance. And right now, things
smelled pretty damn foul on the other end of the line as his father
fed him some fucking rancid story about sending him "help" to
learn the auto shop's finances.

Approximately six months ago, Jackson had purchased the family business, Lancaster's Auto Shop, from his father. He had spent
over a month hospitalized after a motorcycle accident had left him
unable to walk. His recovery process involved the whole family,
with Samantha coming back from Pittsburgh to support him and
assist in his rehabilitation and Dylan covering the shifts at the shop.
Jackson spent a fair amount of his time learning how to walk again,
which made him feel like a goddamn toddler.

It had been a humbling and challenging experience, though
he reasoned he should be grateful that during his downtime, his
younger sister had convinced their father to sell him the shop. With
his dad now free from his responsibilities, he had embarked on a

nomadic journey across America in an RV, seeking self-discovery and engaging in small talk with elderly campers, clutching their yarn and beer while they gossiped by a campfire.

You do you, dad!

Sitting back at his desk, with paperwork spread out around him, he tried to think positively as he responded to his father on the other end of the line. "You know, dad, I think I can figure this shit out on my own." He heard Dylan's snicker across the garage and shot him a dirty look.

"And how long will that take, Jax? Just accept the help." Despite his father's insistence, Jax and his father were cut from the same stubborn cloth, and he knew that neither would back down today.

"Yeah, whatever. Have the guy call me or something." Finally, he agreed, hoping that would be enough to at least bring the conversation to a close. "I'll check my schedule and see what I can do."

The chuckle on the other end of the line annoyed him, as it only meant that dear ole dad was going to do whatever he wanted, anyway. "Yeah, Jax, I'll do that."

"I gotta go. A customer just walked in." Looking up at the empty shop, Dylan stared back at him as he glanced around and rolled his eyes. "I'll talk to you next week." He hung up the phone and groaned, rubbing his palm against his face.

"Smooth." Dylan said with a sarcastic nod. "Sounds like you handled him well."

"Go to hell." Gripping his dirty blonde hair, he stared at the paperwork strewn about his desk and swirled the mouse in his hand as the black screen came back to life. A picture of his sister

Samantha and her boyfriend Blake flashing him the bird, popped up on the monitor. "I need these numbers to make sense before dad gets involved and sends some city slicker suit down here to screw up my life."

"How exactly are you going to do that?" his brother asked, wiping the grease from his forehead with the back of his hand and dropping his screwdriver into the toolbox. "Neither of us even went to city college, man. I have no clue what any of that shit means."

"How hard can it be?" he said, pushing his reading glasses up onto the bridge of his nose. "Dad did it on his own all these years. It can't be that difficult."

"You know, all this time I thought Sam was stubborn, but I think you have her beat." His brother's words were dumb as hell. His sister might be stubborn, but no one was as stubborn as him, and that was an undisputed fact.

He plucked at the keyboard, one finger at a time, his tongue hanging precariously from his mouth, as he tried to enter the purchases for the week. However, the computer kept beeping, an awful sound every time he hit the enter key. He knew he could figure out the damn information if given enough time. He wasn't a complete idiot, but the computer was determined to be his mortal enemy.

"Why does it keep doing that?" He smashed his fist into the keyboard angrily.

Dylan was turning off the lights over the main bay, leaving only a blue Chevy Silverado sitting in the shop that was waiting on parts that wouldn't be arriving until next week. "That's it. Time to get out of here before we need to buy a new computer," Jax growled, ignoring his brother, but Dylan only continued turning off the lights in the garage. "And without even understanding any of that shit, I know we can't afford to buy a new one of those."

"Fine!" Jax said in a frustrated tone. "I need a beer, anyway." He punched his finger against the button on the monitor, causing the screen to turn black. The room was now illuminated only by the soft glow of moonlight streaming through the windows. "You going to Boondocks?" he asked, already knowing the answer.

"Yup." His brother shook his head. "You want me to drive?"

Jax limped slightly, feeling the pain in his hip, the ache in his knee, cursing as he caught up to his brother at the door. Looking over at the motorcycle he was still building to replace the one he had lost in the crash last year, various pieces still stacked precariously in the corner that he had yet to assemble. He sighed. "Yeah, we can take the truck." He tossed the keys at his little brother and shut the door behind him.

Acknowledgements

When I braved the move from fanfiction to the world of creating my own characters, I wasn't sure it was something I was capable of. Luckily, I had the support of some pretty amazing people who helped me gain the confidence I needed to step out on my own.

My husband, Gary, and my daughter Felicia had a front-row seat to all my ramblings and a play-by-play reading of each draft. They assisted in re-writes, helping to come up with character backstories, and constant grumbling from me asking them, "Does it suck?" So much of this book lives within them as much as it does me. I don't think this book would have made it out of my head if not for their constant reassurances. Although, this book also would have ended with Sam and Blake if not for my daughter asking, "But what happens to Jax and Dylan?" So I suppose the fact that this became a three-book series is also her fault, so thanks for that too! In all seriously, thank you both for never letting me quit.

Beyond my family support, I had the support of a friend who reminded me that *comparison is the thief of joy w*hen I told her I was holding back writing my book because I had friends that had written successful books already. Our shared love of Bridgerton and Polin had us spending the last year talking non-stop about writing and fiction. So, when I sat down to start this journey, it was her constant humor and advice that I turned to that kept me going, even on days when I didn't feel like writing. So, thank you, Kara, for your wit, your humor, and your mutual disdain for the same things as me.

I grew up and graduated from the small town of Jefferson, Ohio. So I'm pretty familiar with how small towns work. However, I didn't pick Titusville for any particular reason. Living so close to Pennsylvania as a girl, I could have picked so many towns, but for this book, I literally threw a pin on the map when identifying my small town, USA, home for the Lancasters and Forresters to live in. None of the places or people are real. Boondocks and Linda's Diner do not exist, though the creek and bridges are a beautiful sight to behold.

I do hope anyone from the actual town of Titusville embraced my little family as their own and if not, hopefully they didn't cause too much of a ruckus in book one that you want to kick them to the curb and evict them because Jackson and Dylan have a lot of shenanigans to stir up in book two still.

Thanks again for reading Dragonfly, book one, featuring Samantha Lancaster and Blake Forrester. And though I shed a few tears when the story was done and it was time to write Jackson's tale, I realized how closely knit the family was, so it won't be the last you hear from our couple. Hopefully, you will be just as excited to see what is in store for Jackson and Dylan in the upcoming Lancaster novels, Firefly and Butterfly, coming soon.

About the author

Stacy Goforth was born on the east coast, but spent most of her young life moving from state to state and overseas with her parents. After moving to Arizona as a young adult, she became addicted to the sunshine and the convenience of never needing to set her clock back again and settled down. Now, 20-plus years later, she has grown a life with her husband, four children, one grandchild, two dogs, and two cats.

After spending the last 14 years writing fanfiction for shows like Glee, Once Upon a Time, and Bridgerton, this is her first story created entirely of original characters and ideas. To hear more about her thoughts, writing process, and book ideas, you can join her on the following social media sites:

Instagram *@stacygoforthauthor*

Tumblr: *https://stacygoforthauthor.tumblr.com/*

Facebook: *@stacygoforthauthor*

Website*: https://stacygoforthauthor.com/*

Sign up for this author's newsletter to get exclusive access to the Lancaster and Forrester family tree digital artwork. Joining also gets you access to other exclusive content like bonus chapters, new POV chapters, and other artwork. Join at the following link. https://stacygoforthauthor.eo.page/14716

Content Warnings

This book contains the following content that may be disturbing to some readers: Mention of death of a parent due to an illness (Cancer), mention of death of a parent due to a sudden accident, reference to homophobia, alcohol use, sexual content, and swearing.

www.ingramcontent.com/pod-product-compliance
Lightning Source LLC
Chambersburg PA
CBHW020404110726
47899CB00006B/1857